Books by GEORGE HARMON COXE

Murder with Pictures (1935)
The Barotique Mystery (1936)
The Camera Clue (1937)
Four Frightened Women (1939)
Murder for the Asking (1939)
The Glass Triangle (1939)
The Lady Is Afraid (1940)
No Time to Kill (1941)
Mrs. Murdock Takes a Case
  (1941)
Silent Are the Dead (1942)
Assignment in Guiana (1942)
The Charred Witness (1942)
Alias the Dead (1943)
Murder for Two (1943)
Murder in Havana (1943)
The Groom Lay Dead (1944)
The Jade Venus (1945)
Woman at Bay (1945)
Dangerous Legacy (1946)
The Fifth Key (1947)
Fashioned for Murder (1947)
Venturous Lady (1948)
The Hollow Needle (1948)
Lady Killer (1949)
Inland Passage (1949)
Eye Witness (1950)
The Frightened Fiancée (1950)
The Widow Had a Gun (1951)
The Man Who Died Twice
  (1951)
Never Bet Your Life (1952)
The Crimson Clue (1953)
Uninvited Guest (1953)

Focus on Murder (1954)
Death at the Isthmus (1954)
Top Assignment (1955)
Suddenly a Widow (1956)
Man on a Rope (1956)
Murder on Their Minds (1957)
One Minute Past Eight (1957)
The Impetuous Mistress (1958)
The Big Gamble (1958)
Slack Tide (1959)
Triple Exposure (1959), *containing*
  The Glass Triangle, The Jade
  Venus, *and* The Fifth Key
One Way Out (1960)
The Last Commandment (1960)
Error of Judgment (1961)
Moment of Violence (1961)
The Man Who Died Too Soon
  (1962)
Mission of Fear (1962)
The Hidden Key (1963)
One Hour to Kill (1963)
Deadly Image (1964)
With Intent to Kill (1965)
The Reluctant Heiress (1965)
The Ring of Truth (1966)
The Candid Impostor (1968)
An Easy Way to Go (1969)
Double Identity (1970)
Fenner (1971)
Woman with a Gun (1972)
The Silent Witness (1973)
The Inside Man (1974)
No Place for Murder (1975)

These are Borzoi Books, published in New York by ALFRED A. KNOPF.

NO PLACE
FOR MURDER

NO PLACE FOR MURDER

George Harmon Coxe

ALFRED A. KNOPF, New York, 1975

THIS IS A BORZOI BOOK
PUBLISHED BY ALFRED A. KNOPF, INC.

Copyright © 1975 by George Harmon Coxe

All rights reserved under International and Pan-American Copyright Conventions. Published in the United States by Alfred A. Knopf, Inc., New York, and simultaneously in Canada by Random House of Canada Limited, Toronto. Distributed by Random House, Inc., New York.

Library of Congress Cataloging in Publication Data
Coxe, George Harmon, [Date] No place for murder.
I. Title.
PZ3.C83942Nm   [PS3505.09636]   813'.5'2   75–8239
ISBN 0–394–49768–6

Manufactured in the United States of America

First Edition

For
ASHLEY BUCK

NO PLACE
FOR MURDER

1

Once off the expressway and on the city streets, the Monday morning traffic was still light, and there were plenty of metered parking spaces near the smallish four-storied building where Jack Fenner had his office.

The drive up from Cape Cod had been pleasant and uncomplicated, the late September morning bright and sunny after Sunday's rain. It had been the first fun weekend he'd enjoyed in some time, and the modest profit he had made—five dollars from a back-nine press on the Woods Hole course on Saturday, plus thirty-four from bridge and four-hand stud on Sunday—made the memory even more pleasurable.

Because he did not expect to stay long he put a dime in the meter and swung toward the narrow entrance sandwiched between the book-stationery-greeting-card shop and the travel agency. The building's facade had been sandblasted recently to hide its age. Instead of a street door there was an accordion-type sliding steel gate, locked at night to secure the opening. Beyond was a tunnel-like hallway with a steel fire-door and stairs at the end and, as a concession to modernity, an automatic elevator that could hold two fat people or four thin ones if none of the riders had a claustrophobia hang-up. The small white-on-black directory listed an insurance agency on the second floor; the third was occupied by J. H. FENNER, no occupation listed, two young accountants, a stamp dealer, and an elderly dentist with an all but invisible practice. A firm of architects had the top floor.

Fenner's small suite was across the hall from a similar suite occupied by Fred Lipscomb, the philatelist, and now, reaching for his keys, Fenner inserted the proper one, at the same time twisting the knob from force of habit. When it turned freely and the door gave without the key, he stopped where he was, momentarily surprised and puzzled at his discovery, thinking back, recalling that he had left a little early Friday afternoon but knowing also that Alice Maxwell, his secretary, was careful to make sure that all was properly locked before she left. Slowly then, still wondering, he pushed the door open, eyes busy.

The office beyond would not have suited television's Cannon or Mannix or even Shaft since they all worked out of expensive-looking apartments that were both spacious and luxurious. This one was small, neat, utilitarian.

A waist-high partition in one corner closed off Alice's typewriter desk and chair. The walls were paneled in real wood, though a veneer; there was a good green carpet, four matching maple chairs with cushion seats, a settee of similar construction. A black coffee table held reasonably current copies of *Sports Illustrated*, *Newsweek*, and *Esquire*; there were plenty of ashtrays and two drum lamps on the end tables.

The first thing he noticed as he stood just over the threshold was that one lamp had been knocked to the floor, its wire frame slightly bent. In the same swift glance he saw that an end of the coffee table had been shoved back at an angle. Only when he took his first step did he see the man on the floor, not all of him, just the shoes and trousered legs.

For that first long moment Fenner stood frozen, his reaction one of shock and disbelief. But his early training as a law officer had taught him to resist emotional thoughts and impulses in such situations so he closed off that part of his mind and went quickly around the far end of the coffee table and dropped to one knee beside the head and shoulders of the still figure.

It did not take the blood-soaked collar or the once yellow necktie or the ugly hole just below the Adam's apple to tell him that the man was dead. It was there in the gaunt, tallow-colored face, the unnatural angle of neck and shoulders. Even before he touched the man he knew somehow that he must have been on the settee or in the act of rising when the two slugs hit him from behind. He had fallen or slumped awkwardly between settee and table, in life a man of about Fenner's height—five-eleven or an inch more—skinnier than his own lean, compact build, younger by a few years—maybe thirty-three or so—thinning dark-brown hair, the sizeable moustache looking black against the waxen features.

Still not touching the body, Fenner noticed that a pocket in the trousers of the medium-blue suit had been pulled nearly inside out. After a moment he tapped the inside jacket pocket and found it empty; so were the side pockets. By moving the coffee table an inch or two he was able to reach the twisted hips and knew there was no wallet in the back pockets. Only then did he lift a wrist, replace it. With palms on either side of the long jaw he tested the neck for stiffness. When he finally straightened he knew that the *rigor* period had passed, that the man had been there a long time.

For perhaps five seconds he stood motionless, dark-green gaze fixed but unfocused, his body at ease, the angular jaw slack. Gradually then his mind began to function and he turned slowly until he had inspected every item in the room. Traffic noises filtered up from the street below, but here and in all the building the stillness seemed absolute, and now a delayed reaction came that surprised him a little.

Fenner was not a callous man but he had seen too many dead men, and women—some horribly mutilated—to be unduly moved now. His capacity for pity, for the odd sense of waste and uselessness, had been tarnished; instead there came to him a rising thrust of anger and resentment, not only at the dead man but at the person who had chosen his office as a meeting place for murder.

He stopped first at Alice's desk, deciding to telephone and stop her from coming in. The police would eventually want to question her but they could do that at her place. The electric typewriter bolted to its platform was snugly in the desk compartment, the drawers locked. When he moved to the door of his private office and found it secure, he was satisfied that nothing had been taken. Back at Alice's desk and easing into her chair he dialed her number and she was on the line after the first ring.

"Alice? I'm glad I caught you."

"Oh—Mr. Fenner? I was just leaving. I'm afraid I'll be a few minutes late."

"No, Alice. I want you to stay home this morning."

"Oh?" A pause and he could hear her catch a small breath. "Is—is something wrong?"

Instead of answering directly Fenner told her exactly what he knew in as few sentences as possible, his tone flat and uninflected. Whenever he spoke in that intense determined way he was seldom interrupted and Alice knew him well enough to listen. When he finished the response that came was in character.

For Alice Maxwell was young and blond and bubbly, and sufficiently attractive to have been spoken for by a young doctor in his last year of residency at Massachusetts General. But she was a practical-minded girl with her full share of old-fashioned New England—she came from Vermont—common sense, not given to panic or emotional outbursts. As though to demonstrate these qualities, there was no cry of anguish or horror in her reply. She did not use the Lord's name in any way. The words that finally came were hushed and compassionate and full of understanding.

"How awful for you," she said. "Isn't there anything I can do?"

"Yes, Alice." Fenner kept it businesslike. "The police will probably stop by to question you but that may take some time. So when the stores open duck out and buy a small scatter rug, maybe four-by-six or something like that. Inexpensive but not shoddy. Any pattern you think might look well with that green we have."

"For where?"

"In front of the settee."

"Oh," she said again, voice still soft with understanding. "You mean there'll be—"

"I'm afraid so. Maybe we can have the green one spot-cleaned some time but for now—I mean, that's why I don't want to spend a lot of money."

"All right, Mr. Fenner. Shall I have it delivered?"

"Tell them before five if possible."

He hung up slowly, his bony face wrapped in thought and the eyes still brooding until he remembered the other calls that should be made. As he picked up the handset and began to dial he glanced at his wristwatch, noting the time—8:56.

The first number he dialed connected him with the communications room at police headquarters and he asked for the proper extension, a familiar one by this time. When he had the homicide squad room he identified himself and asked for Lieutenant Bacon because he knew him for what he was—a conscientious, fair-minded, no-nonsense cop whose upward progress in the department had been stymied by a distaste for political games and intrigue.

"Is he in yet?"

"Just now. Hold on."

The gruff impatient voice that came to him had the weary overtones of a man whose application for a loan had been summarily rejected.

"All right, Jack. What is it this time?"

"I think I've got a job for you."

"What do you mean, job? I haven't even got my hat and coat off yet."

"Neither have I. I just got here."

"This job"—there was a definite cadence of doubt in the tone now—"is police business? Somebody rip off your place? Why the hell didn't you call the precinct? You know the routine."

"I didn't call the precinct," Fenner said, "because when I ask for the detectives and get connected, the dick that takes the squeal, it's his case, right? So he and his partner hop over here and ask four hundred questions and they're probably strangers, or maybe one knows me and doesn't like me, and finally they call your office, because like you say that's the routine, and whoever comes over asks the same goddamned questions. I figure it's easier on my disposition to tell it once—to you unless you want to switch me over to Captain Carney."

That got to Bacon in a hurry since there was little love lost between the two men.

"Hold on!" It sounded like a shout, or possibly a snarl. "You're telling me there's a body somewhere."

"A male Caucasian, maybe thirty-two or three. With two slugs in the back of his head. One anyway. I think the other exited."

"All right." The resignation was complete, defeat acknowledged. "Where?"

"My office."

The simple statement brought a pause. When he was ready Bacon tried again, his accents measured, and coldly intent.

"When did you find him?"

"About ten minutes ago. I stopped to pick up Saturday's mail and the outer door was unlocked."

"How long would you say he's been there?"

"Saturday morning."

"What makes you think so?"

"My vast experience with forensic experts—"

"Sure, sure. So go back a step. Stopped in from where? Where were you then? I mean Saturday morning."

"I'll tell you that when you get here."

"You don't know the guy?"

"Nope."

"Didn't check for identification or move the body?"

"I tapped a couple of pockets. I don't think you'll find any identification."

"All right." This time the sigh was audible. "Sit tight and don't snoop."

"You'll call the troops?"

"Oh, shut up!" Bacon said testily, and broke the connection.

Fenner leaned back, the semblance of a humorless grin twisting his mouth, understanding the lieutenant's reaction and grateful for at least some rapport with him. Absently his fingers slid along the hinge of his jaw and he felt the beard there. He realized what his plans had been—to stop briefly for mail and then go on to his place for a shower and shave and a change. The thought of mail made him glance around and survey the floor. There was nothing near the mail slot, which was not surprising with the postal service what it was these days. Deliberately then he concentrated on the two other calls he ought to make.

Because he did not recall the home telephone number of one of the two men—he hoped to catch them before they left for work—he had to unlock Alice's desk and locate her own private directory. With this spread out before him he began once again to dial.

He got Kent Murdock first just as he was about to leave for the *Courier*. He took time for the amenities, and since Murdock knew Fenner had been away for the weekend, he had to go into some detail about what he had done.

With the pleasantries out of the way he said, "The reason I called is I need a favor."

"Sure," Murdock said, "and what else is new?"

"I got a dead man in my office, apparently shot some time Saturday morning. Two in the back of the head. I don't know who he is and I doubt if the police will until they run their fingerprint check. I'm pretty sure he's not local."

Murdock took a silent second or two to digest what he had heard. "Where does the favor come in? I'll phone in and have somebody from the office cover it. Unless the guy turns out to be someone it won't rate much."

"And that's the way I want it. You carry some weight on the *Courier*—I'm going to phone Gene Carter at the *News* as soon as I hang up—and I want you to ask the city editor please not to mention the address or my name. You can see that the story is sort of anonymous, can't you? I mean getting my name in a piece like that might give some prospective client the wrong impression about the kind of people old Jack associates with; it sure as hell won't help business."

"Yeah," Murdock said. "I see what you mean."

"I thought if the story just said 'downtown office building' or something like that it would be enough. Just be sure it don't read, 'the office of Jack Fenner, private investigator.' "

Murdock laughed. "Your point is well taken, Jackson. I'll pass the word. I take it Lieutenant Bacon isn't there yet."

"No, but he's on his way."

"Then you'll have a busy morning. Do you want me to call Gene Carter for you? Bacon's not going to like it if he walks in on you with you on the phone."

Fenner, aware that he had very little time left, thanked his friend and said he appreciated his help.

2

IT TOOK PERHAPS three more minutes for Lieutenant Bacon and his working partner Sergeant Joe Gaynor to arrive. They came quietly, no sirens, no squealing tires so beloved by television directors. Fenner did not even know they were in the building until a discreet knock accompanied the opening of the door.

Fenner had unlocked his private office by then to make sure nothing was missing; now he was back in Alice Maxwell's chair, raincoat still on, the straight black hair, only slightly graying, mussed some above the ears. He met Bacon's fixed long stare with a steady gaze and no word was exchanged for some time as the lieutenant stood unmoving in his first superficial inspection of the man on the floor.

A tall, straight-backed veteran in his early fifties, Bacon had a lean, square-shouldered build with no more than a suggestion of a paunch. There was a craggy corrugated handsomeness to his rectangular face, and as always he wore his own specialized uniform. Except for the polished black oxfords, the white shirt and blue tie, everything was gray—suit, eyes, hair, hat; even his face had a touch of it since it seldom was exposed to bright sunlight. The Gray Lieutenant, Kent Murdock had once called him, and he might have been taken for a banker or a truant officer had it not been for the shrewd observant eyes that seemed always to be estimating, probing, searching, calculating.

Joe Gaynor, much younger, his stockiness contrasting with his superior's spare height, was also more affable by nature. While Bacon was completing his silent inspection the sergeant caught Fenner's eye and gave him a slow wink though his broad face remained dead-pan. When he was close enough he whispered, "Hi." He tipped his chin toward Bacon. "He's not sore, he just don't like to work so early on Mondays."

"Who does?" said Fenner in humorous agreement.

As he spoke Bacon cleared his throat, fanned out his coattails, and hunkered down beside the dead man. He did some things with his hands, his back shielding his movements. Presently his head came up, the immaculate gray hat still dead center, to examine his immediate surroundings. He reached for something beneath the coffee table and stood up. As he turned Fenner saw the spent cartridge shell between thumb and finger.

"A .25," Bacon said. "You wouldn't have one around, would you?" It was just something to say while he organized his thoughts.

"Nope. Two .38's. One here, one at home."

"Yeah. Well, you were going to tell me where you were Saturday."

"Falmouth."

"Doing what?"

"Being a proper houseguest. My host's name was Lathrop."

"Year-round resident?"

"Runs the family lumber business."

"How about Friday night?"

"Same answer."

"When was the last time you were in this office?"

"Around four-fifteen Friday."

Bacon chewed on this a while and changed his approach.

"You don't know this one?" He glanced downward. "Never saw him before?"

"No, and no."

"So you've no idea what he was doing here."

"Not the slightest."

"Well, you could be right about the pockets. He could be clean. We'll know for sure when the m.e. lets us move him."

The door opened before Bacon could continue and two men walked in, strangers to Fenner but at once identifiable to him as city detectives, probably from the precinct. Both were younger than Fenner, one husky, one wiry, dressed in sport coats and slacks. The wiry one wore his brown hair as long as regulations would permit.

The husky one said, "Kelly and Agostino, Lieutenant," and looked down at the body with remarkable disinterest. Bacon did not introduce them. To Fenner he said: ·

"Why don't you park it in that private office of yours? It's going to get crowded in here and you and I have a lot to talk about." Then, as an afterthought, "Oh, yeah. You make any other calls this morning?"

"Two."

Bacon put an upward slant in one graying brow. "Before or after you buzzed me?"

"One before and—"

"Who to?"

"My secretary." He gave her name and address, watching Joe Gaynor write it down.

"Because you wanted to stop her from walking in on this mess?"

"Exactly."

"We'll want to question her. She may have to look at the body."

"I told her that."

"And the other call that came later?"

"To Kent Murdock."

"Oh, for Christ's sake!" Bacon spoke with savage explosiveness and got red in the face. "You got Murdock down here to get some photos for the *Courier* and—"

Fenner, understanding the other's reaction and wanting to be understood, yelled his interruption.

"No such damn thing! I knew there'd be a story on this and I wanted a favor. Murdock carries some clout at the *Courier* and so does Gene Carter at the *News*. Murdock said he would call Carter for me. I told Murdock what had happened and asked him please to get the city editor or the copy desk to keep this address and my name out of it."

"Maybe you told them how to write it?" Bacon was still sore but his tone had been reduced to heavy sarcasm.

"I told them the story wasn't worth more than two paragraphs on page thirteen—unless the guy turns out to be some bigshot—and couldn't they just say that the body of an unidentified man had been found shot twice in the back of the head in a downtown office building and let it go at that."

As he was talking Fenner built up a healthy head of exasperation which needed an immediate outlet.

"By the time you guys spread the word," he added, "every cop in town will know what happened here; so will the whole damn neighborhood. Okay, I can't help that. But I run a legitimate business and I got a reputation to protect and that kind of publicity—a guy shot to death in my office—I don't need. I'll do what I have to do to stop it."

"All right, all right." Bacon recognized a reasonable argument when he heard one. "You've got a point. We'll do what we can to keep your name out of it. Go on now." He turned Fenner gently toward the inner office. "Inside. Simmer down. When we finish the routine out here the sergeant and I'll be in and we'll talk. You want to nail the guy that did this, right? So do we."

The walls in Jack Fenner's room were an extension of the same paneling used in the outer office. The carpet was a similar color but more expensive. There was a good walnut desk, a swivel armchair with a black leather seat. The built-in bookcase was well filled with a variety of books and reference volumes, the bottom shelf none too neat with its stack of magazines. A solid-looking gray steel filing cabinet—fireproof according to the salesman—stood against one wall; there were three walnut armchairs, unpadded, and to the right of the desk, a typewriter stand with a hooded electric portable, a tray, a vacuum carafe, two glasses.

Once in his chair, still wearing the coat, he took out his keys and unlocked the center drawer of his desk. With the locking device released, he opened and closed every drawer, glowering as he did so, not looking for anything but making noises and venting his irritation like a spoiled child.

He knew his mood was sullen and foul, his rage directed not at Bacon or the specialists that would make a mess of the outer office before they left, but focused as much on his own sense of futility as on the unwarranted conclusion that the whole operation, the murder included, had been aimed at him personally. Now, banished, practically dispossessed, he felt like a man who, having built a prosperous business, had just been kicked out of the presidency by the vote of dissenting board members.

But he also had the resiliency of all professionals, and such brooding could not be maintained when things began happening beyond the still-open door. His native curiosity and his long cultivated interest in police procedure overcame the temporary feeling of abandonment and he finally sat up, eyes watchful and ears finely tuned to voices and movement.

Bright lights that flashed intermittently told him a police photographer was at work. He lost track of new arrivals since he could not see the outer door, but soon another specialist moved into view and began to work with his brushes and powders and spray can; another operator with a fingerprint camera followed him around. He also got a glimpse of the arriving deputy medical examiner, a man he knew but could not name, a slight quick-moving fellow with wispy hair and metal-rimmed spectacles. Bacon moved into view for quick consultation before the doctor stepped from sight.

For perhaps five minutes Fenner sat like an obedient schoolboy, imagination working and impatience mounting until, finally, he swore softly and rose out of the chair, annoyed that he had taken his banishment so literally. Once established and leaning comfortably against the doorframe he became aware of other movement but his attention was glued on the examiner's man, who was just coming to his feet.

Bacon was waiting for the verdict, coattails fanned out and hands on hips. The voices of others in the room prevented Fenner from getting all the words but he did hear enough to corroborate at least one of his guesses.

"So you put it forty-eight hours?" Bacon said.

"Give or take a few."

At which announcement Fenner gave a silent but exultant *"Hah!"*

"Saturday morning." Bacon again. "Not Friday night maybe?"

"Doubt it." The doctor clung to his estimate as he slipped on his coat. "Stomach contents should tell us something. If we find the residue of breakfast—"

Fenner lost the next few words; then, "Not contact?"

"Definitely not, but close. Signs of singeing on the hair. I'd say twelve inches or less."

Fenner watched the examiner leave but when the ambulance attendants bustled in a couple of minutes later he went back to his desk chair and eased into it. He was still there, motionless and stone-faced, when Bacon and Sergeant Gaynor came in. This time the lieutenant closed the door, glanced around, selected one of the armchairs, motioning Gaynor to do the same.

Still not saying anything, he brought out a long, thin, poisonous-looking cigar that until recently would have been called a stogy. He took care in lighting it, placed the used match in a desk ashtray. When he was ready he said:

"Okay, we've got to start somewhere. The nature of the wounds say it was a professional hit, but it doesn't have to be. Either way, why was your office picked?"

He did not really expect an answer and Fenner's shrug was enough.

"Coincidence? I don't think so. This office was picked because the hit man knew the victim would not be discovered until two days after the job was done. Also you were right about the pockets. Empty. To delay identification? . . . Not if the victim has a record. We took a full set of prints and they'll go out over the wire and while we're checking so will the New York City boys and the F.B.I."

"Why New York?"

"The jacket had a label from a New York City store. So who'd know your office would stay empty? You know any reason for somebody setting you up? You had any little disagreement with the local mob or the Mafia?"

"None."

"You left here around four-fifteen on Friday?"

"Right."

"Your girl—what's her name again?—locked up?"

Fenner nodded.

"You drove to the Cape from here?"

"Right. I had my bag and golf sticks in the car."

"So what happened between Friday afternoon and this morning?"

Fenner tried to be patient. He knew that Bacon did not suspect him; he also knew by the very nature of police investigation that questions had to be asked and routine followed by any thorough officer, since there was always a chance that out of that routine would come an incident, a bit of information that, when coupled with other bits, might result in a worthwhile lead.

He kept the story chronological, starting with the small dinner party at his host's home. He mentioned the golf game at

Woods Hole, naming the other two members of the foursome. At this point Bacon interrupted.

"These other two guys, they residents of Falmouth too?"

"Not Larsen. He has a summer home. Works for an ad agency in New York but comes up weekends until it gets cold. It was his forty-five-foot Hatteras we went fishing with on Sunday, only it rained and we didn't do much fishing."

"What's a Hatteras, some kind of boat?"

Fenner laughed for the first time that morning. "Some kind of boat is right. If you had maybe a hundred grand, give or take a few odd thousand, you might buy one new, depending on how much electronic gear you wanted to pay for."

Bacon's reaction was a rare one: he showed surprise.

"A hundred thousand? Jesus! Some friends you have."

"A friend of a friend," Fenner said. "I'd never met the guy before."

He went on without prodding to tell of the brief spell of fishing which resulted in two bonita, the decision to forget fishing; the trip to Cuttyhunk where they had drinks and lunch, the hours of card games and more drinks that followed in the steady rain, until it was time to head back along the Elizabeth Islands for Nobska Light and finally the narrow safety of Falmouth harbor.

He said to repay in some measure the hospitality extended he had taken the men and their wives to dinner at Coonamessett Inn and had slept aboard the boat because he wanted an early start and did not want his host and hostess to think they had to get up and give him breakfast.

"That's why I haven't shaved," he said. "I made a cup of instant and took off."

Bacon, who had been nodding from time to time, very thoughtful but without any visible reaction, looked over at Gaynor, who had been making notes.

"Joe," he said dryly, "you ever spend a weekend like that? Think we ever will?"

"We don't know the right kind of people."

"Yeah." Bacon examined the end of his cigar, tapped the growing ash. "So who knew you'd be gone?"

Fenner, who had been readying himself for the question for some time, sighed audibly, tipped one hand, spoke glumly, the green eyes troubled.

"Fifteen or twenty people probably."

"Start with the Maxwell girl. She got boyfriends?"

Fenner said one, and named him.

"Who'd you tell in the building?"

"Old man Lipscomb across the hall."

"The stamp guy? Anybody else?"

"Marge Tyler, the redhead down in the travel agency. She could have told the others. . . . Saul Klinger. Owns the delicatessen across the street—his daughter, son-in-law, Eddie the delivery boy . . . Moe—I don't know his last name—one of the cab drivers that uses the stand around the corner."

He stopped then, brows warped, both eyes squinting at nothing as his brain picked up and replayed a scene he had all but forgotten. It was, he knew, absurd even to mention it but he realized it was better to tell it all rather than be accused later of holding something back.

"Alan Townsend knew."

"What Townsend is that?"

"Carter and Townsend."

"The stockbrokers? How come? You got an account there? Big enough for one of the partners to handle it?"

"Cut it out!" Fenner said, aware that Bacon was gently needling him but in no mood for banter. "An account executive, or customer's man, or whatever they call them now named George Abbott takes care of me. But I did a job for Alan Townsend a year or so ago and we've been sort of friendly since."

Bacon thought it over, head tipped, not looking at Fenner now, the gray eyes narrowed in thought. To prove that he read the newspapers he finally said:

"One of those Townsends got a divorce about that time. You

involved?" When Fenner nodded he added, "I thought you ducked divorce work."

"I do," Fenner said. "If you mean keyhole-peeping and busting in motel rooms with a camera. This came from Townsend's lawyers and was very neat and clean. You want to know how?"

"I got time." Bacon cocked an eye at Gaynor. "Okay with you, Joe?"

Fenner stared at him, no longer amused. "You know something, Lieutenant? Keep on with that and I won't tell you a goddamned thing."

"Okay, okay." For once Bacon looked mildly repentant. "It's just that I'm seeing a new side of you. Golf at Woods Hole, hundred-grand yachts, buddy-buddy with bigshot brokers. Go ahead. How did it work?"

"Alan is a very fine gentleman. Very proper. Some might say a bit stuffy. Just the sort that sometimes marries a society swinger, and this one had the morals of an alley cat. Alan had warned her before and this time he even knew who the guy was. So I got some help. It wasn't hard to pick up a line on the two of them but what tore it was when the wife decided a weekend in Puerto Rico with the boyfriend might be fun."

He grunted softly and said, "Got pictures of the two of them boarding the plane. Passenger manifest, the guy's right name. They have private investigators in San Juan, too, you know, so I made a couple of calls. Photos of them arriving at the hotel, a peek at the registration card. My man was waiting here with a camera when they arrived at Logan Sunday night."

"Neat." Bacon nodded approvingly. "So how'd you happen to tell Townsend about this weekend?"

"I stopped in the office to see my guy Abbott about a couple of things and Townsend saw me—"

"When was this?"

"Thursday afternoon. So Townsend takes me into his office." Fenner eyed Bacon aslant, a grin working on his mouth. "On account I'm such a valued customer."

"Sure, sure."

"Now are you ready for a bit of coincidence?"

"If you can make me believe it."

"Well, we're sitting there talking about this and that and the phone rings. From what I hear it sounds like somebody's breaking a date, which is what happened."

"This is important?" Bacon fidgeted, his sigh suggesting either boredom or some minor suffering.

"You asked me who knew—"

"All right. Forgive me. Get on with it."

"Alan Townsend has a regular golfing foursome every Saturday at Braeburn and one of the members had to cancel. Alan knows I'm a twelve because I played with him once before so he asks if I want to fill in. I tell him no, and why, and where I'm going, so he asks his brother in."

"What's the brother's name?"

"Bruce. A few years younger. Used to play quarterback at Harvard and—"

"Hold it." Bacon's gray gaze narrowed and he stared off into space before he continued. "Didn't I hear a rumor that *this* Townsend's marriage is also in trouble, that he moved out on his wife?"

"You could have, because he did."

"Those Townsends have some track record. Didn't the old man have three or four wives?"

"Three." Fenner waited until he had Bacon's attention. "So Alan asks Bruce to fill in and Bruce says he has a date and when I left Alan was on the phone again still trying to get a fourth."

"So those two knew your office would be empty."

"And my customer's man, George Abbott. If you want me to guess who they might also have told, or who Saul Klinger's delicatessen bunch told, I pass."

Bacon sighed again. He had been watching Gaynor write all this down and now he stood up and shrugged his coat collar into place.

"Zilch, right?" he said. "As far as tying any of them into the murder."

"Until you identify the victim," Fenner replied, "I'd say yes."

Bacon opened the door, let Gaynor move in front of him, then turned back. "I guess you'll be asking some questions of your own. You know, around? Tenants, your neighborhood pals."

"You know I will," Fenner said, and again there was a harshness in his tone. "Some bastard has made a lot of trouble for me, maybe deliberate, maybe not. I intend to spend some time on it."

"Maybe you can dig up a client to help pay for your time. You usually do."

Fenner started to answer but the words that came to mind were mostly profane so he clamped his lips tight and stayed mute until he heard the outer door close.

3

NORMALLY JACK FENNER did not use his car in the city, what with the short-term meters and the high-rise garages where bent fenders were more common than traffic tickets. Instead he patronized a smaller neighborhood garage about halfway between his office and his apartment. On nice days he could walk either way; when the weather was inclement, or worse, he could usually have it delivered for a dollar or two.

Now, moving uncertainly toward his four-door and still undecided as to what he wanted to do first, he saw that one of the city's notoriously incorrupt and unreasonable meter maids had already been at work. A ticket had been slipped under one wiper blade and he glared at it, muttering, started to remove it, then changed his mind. He was going to have to pay for the space anyway now so why the hell not keep it until he was ready to move?

This decision ruled out the shave and shower temporarily. He had already called the janitor service and extracted a promise to send a crew around to clean up the mess left in his office by the headquarters technical crew. Now he began to concentrate on possible witnesses who might have been watching the building entrance on Saturday morning.

The upper-floor tenants he ruled out for now, since few if any were open on Saturday. Only Fred Lipscomb occasionally stopped in to bring his records up to date and he could talk to him any time. The bookstore was out, its display window so full of the latest best seller that had to be pushed as to make it impossible for anyone to see in or out. That left the travel agency and Klinger's Delicatessen.

What decided him was the sudden awareness of some acrobatic activity behind the agency window. The lower half of the pane had a sloping counter or shelf where a variety of colorful travel folders, cutouts, and maps were spread; above it, motioning through the glass in wild, near-panic gestures, was Marge Tyler. When she caught his eye her red mouth formed silent phrases but the hand signals beckoned unmistakably. He knew instantly what she wanted and what awaited him once he entered—questions, and more questions. For almost certainly she knew what had happened and had perhaps been questioned by one of Bacon's men. So all right. Since he had a few questions of his own, he gave her a smiling salute and started inside.

It was a narrow but rather deep layout, with a counter partway down the left side and a few chairs lined up against the opposite wall where surplus customers, if any, could wait their turn, meanwhile consulting travel literature of nearly any desired kind. A door in the rear wall gave on another office, unknown to the general public. It was this smaller office that paid much of the rent and it dealt in only one sort of travel service—charter flights to Las Vegas and various Caribbean islands offering wide-open gambling, its customers anyone whose credit had been established beforehand and could be counted on to make good their losses or be prepared to pay an outrageous weekly interest rate.

At this hour there were no prospects for travel, just Marge, plus a middle-aged and graying lady with a severe but not forbidding countenance and, at a desk near the rear, the manager. From Fenner's observation the duties of each were well defined. Marge Tyler was the front woman, the greeter, and she was good at it. A twenty-six-year-old divorcee who was waiting for a firm offer from any qualified applicant for the number two spot, she had thick auburn hair, a ripe, firmly-rounded figure, and a practiced smile. The proper makeup enhanced a certain basic attractiveness, adding allure to friendly greenish eyes that she knew how to use. More important she had the ability to distinguish and separate quickly the active prospects from the potentials and the dreamers.

When Marge thought it appropriate she would pass the potential client along to Miss Asnip, who had specific facts, figures, airline schedules, and hotel rates. Mr. Harris, the manager, a small, neat man with the firm but unctuous manner of an assistant funeral director, issued the necessary tickets and confirmations, and collected payment.

Now, in spite of an obvious air of urgency and excitement, Marge's opening remark was characteristic and unflattering.

"Hi, Jack. You need a shave."

"I know," Fenner said. "I hope to get one before the day is over. You don't have an electric one under the counter, do you?"

Ignoring this she said, "And is it true"—the eyes were wide open now, the voice hushed—"that you walked in your office and found a dead man?"

"I sure did."

"Right there on the floor?"

"Right there on the floor."

"Shot?"

"Twice."

His replies to the questions that followed were brief but factual and when he had a chance he said, "I take it the law has been here."

"Oh, yes. Two of them."

"What did they want to know?"

"How long we were open Saturdays. I told them noon. About the other tenants. You know, who usually came in Saturdays and did I see any of them last Saturday."

"And did you?"

"Only Mr. Lipscomb."

"Was it a busy morning here?"

"Saturday was dead," Marge said disgustedly. "One young couple. Engaged. I think we sold them a week in Bermuda for a honeymoon."

"So you had plenty of time to daydream and stare out the window."

"What else?"

"So who, I mean beside Lipscomb, did you see that looked as if he might be coming next door? There must have been somebody."

She took her time with this one, head cocked slightly and a frown topping the thoughtful, mascaraed eyes.

"Well, yeah. Come to think of it." She thought some more. "One guy—I think he was the first one I saw after Mr. Lipscomb—was a tall, thin fellow, not much to look at so I didn't give him a lot of time."

"What *do* you remember?"

"Had a long, hollow-looking face. Flashy dresser—blue suit and shirt and a yellow tie, but no class. You know, a race-track type; a small-time hustler, is what I thought. Carried a raincoat over one arm and, oh yeah, a brown envelope in his hand."

It was a pretty good description and Fenner recognized it. Belatedly then Marge seemed to realize she might have been describing a dead man and for a moment her jaw was slack with wonderment.

"Jesus!" she breathed. "Could that have been—I mean, don't tell me he's the one—"

She could not get it all out and Fenner helped her.

"I'm afraid so, Marge. The description fits."

She let her breath out, deflating a noteworthy bosom. Before she could think of an appropriate comment Fenner said:

"Who else? Think hard."

She seemed to be doing just that, the frown deepening. Then, just as suddenly, her face cleared and a smile came.

"There was another fellow. At least I think he turned in there. I didn't see him leave."

"What made you notice him?"

"Because he was dreamy."

"Dreamy?" Fenner said, suppressing a grin.

"You know, tall, thick blondish hair, good build. A real handsome guy, big too. Looked like he was in the chips. I just happened to see him get out of a sports car across the street, down a ways from Klinger's."

"What kind of a sports car?"

"Foreign. I don't know the makes. A low one, medium-gray." She was picking up enthusiasm as her imagination re-created the moment. "I moved over to the window, hoping he'd look in and see me," she added with diminishing interest.

"And did he?"

"Did he what?"

"Look at you?"

"Oh, sure. Right through me, if he saw me at all. I don't think it was a brush-off; I don't think he even knew I was there."

Fenner filed away the description even though he did not know if such knowledge would ever help.

"You'd know him if you saw him again?"

"I sure would."

Fenner offered a cigarette and a light, his faint smile fixed but encouraging. "Did dreamboat come in before or after the hustler?"

"After. I meant to watch him leave but maybe I was talking to the Bermuda couple. They were in about then."

"Who else might have come up?"

"A girl, I think. I mean she was headed that way. Young, twenty or so, dark hair, sort of pageboy. Wore a print dress with a cardigan; a short skirt but good legs." She thought some more, brow puckering and distance growing in her gaze. "There could have been a hippie type, too. I had the feeling he'd just come from next door but I wouldn't swear to it. Tight black slacks and a short brown coat. Straight black hair, shoulder length or longer, blue sneakers. Never saw the face; he'd already turned away when I spotted him. If it was a he. How can you tell these days. Some of 'em even wear pigtails, I mean the guys, right?"

Fenner pushed away from the counter and glanced at the closed door at the rear. "The charter boys in Saturday?"

"No. Not before we closed anyway. Charlie was away somewhere rounding up a new cargo of suckers. I don't know where Max was. Out collecting maybe."

Klinger's Delicatessen had its counterpart in most sizeable towns and was typical of neighborhood delicatessens in metropolitan areas all over the East. A family operation, it had been a matriarchy until Mrs. Klinger had died a couple of years earlier; now Saul gloried in his advancement from counterman to proprietor and took delight in shouting orders from his cashier's stool in the front window to show his authority.

A widowed sister ran the kitchen, roasting and baking and mixing the potato salad and coleslaw. The daughter, Sheila, an attractive, bright-eyed, and energetic brunette, was assisted in dispensing orders by her harried and taciturn husband, who, at thirty, had the air of a man who had already given the best years of his life to the business.

The interior had the narrowness of the travel agency, and its odors, which had permeated the walls and ceiling, while undefinable, were aromatic and decidedly appetizing. Glass showcases on the left held the goodies. The wall shelves were lined with staples. There were six small tables, each with four chairs, opposite the counter but there was no table service. You stood at the counter until your order was filled and carried it to whatever table space was available; once in a while

Eddie, the towheaded delivery boy, collected the dishes and wiped the tops.

The lunch hours were the busy time. For a couple of hours the chairs were continually occupied, and while the price of a sandwich seemed outrageous by comparison with the hamburg chains, what one got was a hearty made-to-order masterpiece with an unlimited variety of ingredients. Other than side orders of salad or coleslaw and a soup *du jour,* that was it. Breakfast was limited to juice, freshly baked Danish, dough-nuts, and coffee. The late afternoon and early evening business was mostly of the take-out variety.

Apparently having seen Jack Fenner cross the street, Saul Klinger was ready for him. It was too late for breakfast and somewhat early for lunch and Saul, a paunchy man of sixty or so with thick graying hair, had time on his hands; bushy brows hooded the small bright eyes and he had a practiced scowl that he used to mask an outgoing and basically friendly nature.

"So," he said, pulling Fenner close to his throne by the window, "you had trouble at your place this morning. You got ideas why a thing like that would happen in your office?"

"Not yet. But I'm working on it. You know everything that goes on in the street. Tell me who you saw go in or out of my building Saturday morning."

"You mean besides Lipscomb who belongs there?"

"Right." Fenner gestured across the street. "Marge Tyler over at the travel place remembers four."

"Four? Hmmm. I didn't count. I'm not keeping score, just looking because business is lousy."

"She says one was a thin guy in a blue suit, carrying a coat."

"Him I remember." Klinger nodded judiciously. "Comes maybe a half hour after Lipscomb."

"What time would that be?"

"Ten. Maybe before maybe after. I never did see him come out."

"Yes, you did."

The bushy brows climbed. "I did?"

"If you were looking. On a stretcher."

Klinger blinked once, said, "Oy—" and clapped one palm to his forehead, his expression more curious and anticipatory than horrified. "And this skinny fellow is shot to death in your office is why I didn't see him come out?"

"That's how it looks, Saul. So who else? Marge says a tall good-looking dude."

"Him too, I remember. A rich sport."

"What makes him rich?"

"He wears slacks and a woolly expensive sport coat. What makes him rich is he's got these leather patches sewn on the elbows. A poor man, he throws away his coat when it comes out at the elbows. Bigshots sew patches. Maybe on account of the coat costs so much in the first place."

Fenner suppressed a chuckle at Klinger's conclusion and kept pressing.

"Did you see him come out?"

"No."

"This hippie type, Marge spoke of. Male or female?"

"Who knows? Like the other day. I'm walking along Boylston and ahead of me is this girl. Pants, straight legs, a tight little behind. Straight long blond hair, nice and shiny in the sun. And it makes me want better to see the face that goes with this nice figure. So I hurry a little. When I get past to give her a smile what do I see?"

"A moustache," Fenner said, taking a guess.

"Correct. And one of these." He stroked the point of his chin between thumb and forefinger.

"A goatee."

"So how can I tell when I don't see the face. But the other, that one I'm sure is a girl. I see her come out. This is after I see Mister Sport. When she's on the sidewalk she looks like she can't make up her mind which way to go. That's how I got a look at her. Not tall, not short, dark glasses, short skirt and sweater, a cute figure."

"So?" Fenner prompted when Klinger paused. "What did she do?"

"Goes to the corner by the bookstore. Then she spots the taxi. She goes over and leans in the front window to say something to the driver; then she climbs in back."

It was then that Fenner realized he might have some sort of a lead. For while the space in the two-cab stand beyond the corner was available to any licensed hack, its regular patrons were two drivers named Moe and Lonny. Because he used them regularly Fenner opened the door and started out, hearing Klinger's loud entreaties and complaints but not understanding a word he said.

There was a cab at the curb when Fenner got there, its owner-driver a squat jowly character of indeterminate age. He always wore a cap to cover his baldness, and like so many drivers he was as garrulous and independent as he was argumentative. His first name was Moe, the last one an unlikely sequence of letters that Fenner had never tried to pronounce. Moe's greeting was gruffly cheerful.

"Morning, Mr. Fenner. I heard about the excitement and it's just my luck to come in late. You know, Monday morning blues. Is it true there was a stiff in your office?"

Fenner nodded, containing his impatience.

"And still unidentified?" Moe pressed. "Why the hell should he pick your office if you don't even know him?" He would have said more but Fenner put one hand firmly on Moe's forearm and interrupted bluntly.

"Look, Moe. Up to now I don't know from nothing. When I get a clue, or the cops do, I'll fill you in on my next ride, okay? Now, were you on duty Saturday morning?"

"No. I have to take the wife shopping, the kids for new shoes and her for groceries. But Lonny was; least he said he'd be. Hey! You think he might have seen the guy that did the job?"

"When will he be back, do you know?"

"Shouldn't be too long. You want to quiz him?"

Ignoring the question this time Fenner said: "I'll be over at Klinger's. When Lonny shows ask him to hop over a minute, okay?"

Back at Klinger's, Fenner tried to think what he could put in his stomach. It was too late for breakfast and he was in no mood to consider lunch. Not really hungry but with an emptiness inside him he wondered about a dish of dry cereal and milk; then an impulse that sprang from nowhere made him ask about the soup of the day. When Sheila told him minestrone he ordered a bowl. He was just finishing it when a shadow moved at his elbow and Lonny Parks slid onto the chair opposite him.

A slender, lithe-looking black, smooth-shaven and neat in his tan slacks and windbreaker, Lonny wore his hair in a modest Afro and always drove bareheaded because, he said, "Anybody flags me down has a right to know who he's got for a driver; he don't like blacks he can wave me on."

Now, getting comfortable, he said, "Greetings. Moe says I was to stop in. You thinking of a trip"—his perfect teeth gleamed whitely in his grin—"like maybe down to Providence and back? It's a nice day for it."

Fenner gave him a tight smile, held up his right hand, and slowly crossed the first two fingers for luck. He let Lonny understand the sign before he spoke.

"Saul says he thinks maybe you hauled a young lady Saturday morning. Somebody did, and if you were parked there—"

"Could have. Is it about the killing?"

Fenner pretended he hadn't heard. "Young, short skirt, dark hair, glasses. Maybe around ten-thirty to eleven Saturday."

Lonny nodded. "Saul is right. I remember the dress. Figured, summery, short, with a cardigan. Showed a lot of thigh climbing in back. Very nice. Neat figure, cute nose. Couldn't see the eyes because of the shades. Real pale in the face though. If I was to guess I'd say she was in kind of shock, you know, real scared. Also strictly uncommunicative after she asks do I know where the Starlight Motel is."

"What do you mean, uncommunicative?"

"I say, 'Good morning.' No answer. I say, 'Are you a stranger in town, Miss?' Same nothing. Not a damn word until she tells me to pull up in front of unit sixteen and asks how much for the trip."

Fenner heard all this but now his mind was concentrating in another direction. He had uttered a not altogether silent sigh of relief as he understood he really could have a potential lead, but he still could not place the motel. What with all the mushrooming of new ventures in the not too distant past on the outskirts of the city and suburbs, a man needed a directory and he said so.

"Starlight? I've seen it—"

"An old type. One story. Out by the B.U. field on the old road."

"Ahh—" Fenner took another satisfied breath as the first stirrings of some new excitement expanded swiftly within him. "Got it," he said, and after a bit of fumbling started to slide a five-dollar bill across the table.

Lonny stopped him with one hand and shook his head.

"Forget it, man. A small favor now and then for a regular customer is all part of Lonny Parks's deluxe service. Especially good tippers, you know?"

He pushed back his chair and stood up. He said he'd be around. Maybe Fenner would let him know how he, Fenner, made out with the chick.

"The only thing," he added realistically, dampening somewhat Fenner's incipient hopefulness, "is that this trip was two days ago, you dig? To old Lonny it seems like you're going to have to be mighty lucky if you make a connection."

4

THE STARLIGHT MOTEL was as Lonny Parks had described it and only great good luck and a fortunate bit of highway planning had enabled it to survive. For the motel had been constructed long before the city planners or the highway department even had the expressway on the drawing board. As it was there was a Turnpike exit ramp within a block and a half of the motel which made it convenient to reach if one took the right turn. Modest rates apparently kept it solvent.

Built entirely of red brick, with white trim that showed signs of flaking, it had a two-story center unit—reception and coffee shop downstairs and the owner's or manager's quarters above—and was shaped like a broad-based U. Thirty units, Fenner discovered. Nine on either side of the center unit and six on each side of the U.

Checking numbers as he idled his car into the parking area, he found number 16 on the right front, one door away from the corner. Three cars parked along the front suggested there were still some late check-outs, but the space allotted to 16 was unoccupied and Fenner nosed in and cut the motor.

Leaning back in the new silence, he got a cigarette going and began to consider alternatives and possibilities, none of them encouraging. For Lonny Parks's final words had planted a small but annoying burr that clung irritably in the back of his brain. A young lady, a likely lead if one threw out coincidence and stuck to acceptable suppositions, had been driven here last Saturday morning. In all probability she had been registered the previous afternoon or evening.

That she would still be here, particularly if she were in any way involved in murder, was highly unlikely. The empty parking space seemed to say so. Of course there was a registration card and information to be had if one made a proper approach to the front desk and found a cooperative clerk who was not averse to trading information for a suitable fee.

But Jack Fenner had been in the business too long to overlook even remote possibilities and he had been endowed with a native stubbornness to augment his experience. Now, moving from the front seat to the walk, he considered ways of entering unit 16. Empty or not, he wanted a look. He carried a sophisticated gadget that would take care of the lock but this could take a minute or so, and while there was no one in sight out front, he took time to move to his right and glance down that side of the building. He was glad he did because a laundry cart stood in front of the second door down. Three steps told him the door was open so he reached in and knocked. Presently a plump but tired-looking black woman appeared.

Fenner offered an apologetic smile and spoke convincingly. "I wonder if you could let me into sixteen. I don't want to walk all the way back to the desk for my key. I'll only be a couple of minutes and I'd appreciate it."

"Check-out time's noon," she complained. "I got to get my work done."

But she was already eyeing the folded dollar bill, and when he repeated he'd only be a couple of minutes she accepted the gratuity and led the way.

The hope that had been deteriorating swiftly since Fenner's arrival got a quick new lift when he stepped inside and took his first look around. For while there was no one in the room, the open suitcase on the bed was proof that the tenant—whoever he or she might be—had not yet checked out.

Compared with the present-day decor offered by the chain motels, the room bore incontestable marks of long usage. The walls were a sickly green, the only decoration a print of a still-life in a cheap frame between the twin beds. The carpet was well worn and nearly threadbare in spots; the bedspreads had tiny mends. The only concession to the times was a fairly new television set with an eighteen-inch screen.

Although Fenner catalogued all this in his first sweeping glance, his attention riveted on the suitcase on the nearest bed, a lightweight imitation case of cheap construction. Under-things, a filmy robe, and cheap scuffs had been deposited in the bottom compartment, and toilet articles in a waterproof pouch had been placed nearby along with two dresses, a print and a plain black, neither yet folded. Aside from medium-heeled pumps there was nothing else in sight, and Fenner began opening drawers on his way to the recessed clothes alcove with its theft-proof hangers.

The bedside table drawer was empty. Those in the combination dresser and vanity held only a Gideon, but two ashtrays were well filled with cigarette butts, the filtered ends red-stained. The closet area proved more productive. On the floor, next to a pair of loafers, was a tan suitcase which, when opened, revealed nothing more than two soiled shirts, blue socks, a pair of shorts. A raincoat, more wrinkled than Columbo's, hung from one hanger; next to it was a tan suit and finally a pair of gray-flannel slacks.

The bathroom yielded nothing helpful and Fenner turned back to the tan suit. All trouser pockets were empty except for a wadded handkerchief. One side jacket pocket contained some tobacco shreds in the bottom welt and the other had two folders of paper matches. One said *Starlight Motel*, the other was a nightclub throwaway with an unfamiliar name. Only when he patted the inside pocket and heard the crackle of paper did he discover anything of interest.

This was, he saw, a plain, letter-size sheet of thin bond—a carbon copy—that made little sense to Fenner at first glance.

He was aware of two long columns, one of letters in two- and three-letter combinations, the other a list of figures ranging from 200 to 1,800.

Then, just as he began to consider the significance of his discovery, he heard the key in the door and time ran out.

There was a second to wonder if he had half-consciously heard any car stop outside, to ask himself if he should have been more prepared, not that it mattered now. As the door started to swing he did the only thing he could—jammed the sheet in his left-hand jacket pocket, having no time to refold it. He saw her come in and had time to step back from the hangers before she looked up and saw him.

For perhaps six silent seconds they stood as they were, neither moving as the tension built, more than time enough for Fenner to understand that this was the young woman Saul Klinger and Lonny Parks had described. The only apparent difference was in her outfit, which now consisted of a plaid wool skirt, a white jersey, and a tan cardigan. Fenner, not wanting to startle her further, let her make the first move.

It came a moment later.

Unhurried, no sign of panic showing, she kicked the door shut behind her and snapped open her handbag. With almost studied deliberation she thrust one hand inside. When it reappeared she was pointing a revolver with a two-inch barrel. The muzzle seen from Fenner's distance suggested a .32 or .38 caliber.

Still careful, she reached sideways to a round magazine table, the kind with a lamp standard thrusting upward from its center, and put the handbag down. While she was considering her next move Fenner had time to catalogue mentally sufficient physical characteristics to file a missing persons report.

The figure, even in the sweater, was neat and nicely proportioned. Five-foot-five or six, he guessed; a hundred and fifteen pounds. No beauty but attractively feminine nonetheless. Mahogany-colored hair shorter than most these days, the generous mouth dipping at the corners now and very tight. Small snub nose, the smooth complexion having a pale indoor cast. He could not see her eyes behind the dark glasses but a certain worn look at the corners gave the impression of an eighteen-year-old who looked more like twenty-five. When she finally spoke her voice was cold, curious, emotionless.

"Fuzz?"

Fenner's narrowed green gaze was speculative but friendly; his attitude was one of apology and innocence.

"Fuzz? Do I look like fuzz?"

"Not exactly."

"So why should fuzz be interested in you or your room?"

"You don't look like a rip-off creep."

"If the real fuzz *was* looking for you," he said, ignoring her last remark, "maybe it's because they found out you were seen downtown Saturday outside an office building where an unidentified man was found shot to death this morning. They might also be wondering if maybe the victim was a friend of yours."

That got to her. He could still not see her eyes behind the brown lenses but he noticed the facial spasm, the parted lips, the perceptible stiffening of her body and stance. When he saw the reaction tighten her grip on the gun butt, he continued quickly.

"No fuzz," he said. "Private."

"So prove it."

"Sure." Fenner reached for his hip and she stopped him.

"Hold it. Fan out that coat. Your jacket too. Let's have a look."

Fenner did as directed. "No gun," he said, and reached back to extract his wallet.

"On the bureau. Easy."

She watched carefully as he obeyed. He could see her glance moving from side to side as if searching for something in the room. When she finally made up her mind, he knew she had been seeking some means to immobilize him effectively and he admitted her method was cute.

"Move over behind that second bed and flop down on it. On your back. Yeah. That's it. . . . How about clasping your hands behind your neck." She indicated the gun. "I'm no expert with this thing but I guess I could score somewhere."

Carefully, then, she moved to the dresser, examined the open wallet.

"So you really are private. Who you working for?"

"Myself at the moment."

"Why? What's your angle?"

"The guy who got himself killed picked my office. I want to know why and how and who. You were there. You could have cleaned out his pockets, hoping he'd be unidentified for a while."

Ignoring such reasoning and making no comment, she removed the dark glasses revealing somehow a look of disillusionment and defeat. Hazel, he thought. Large, too, and well spaced, with little or no makeup. But still watchful and full of thought as she considered her next move. What she said surprised him a little.

"I have to change," she said. "I was up to Howard Johnson's for a bite. Came back just in time, didn't I?" She moved to the bed near the door and turned the suitcase so she could continue her packing.

Still holding the gun she used her free hand to work a zipper on her skirt. A few twists and wiggles of the hips and it slipped to the floor and she stepped out of it, flipped it up with a toe and caught it with her left hand. Still with one hand she unbuttoned the cardigan, shrugging first one arm and then the other out of it. She had a bit more trouble with the jersey. She had to put the gun down for a couple of seconds but it was never more than inches away.

Fenner watched with a growing fascination. Although she could not know it, she had nothing to worry about insofar as he was concerned. He was content to observe and speculate and though he understood her wariness, her concern with the gun, such caution was unnecessary since he had no intention of making any move in that direction. For he had faced guns before and could discriminate between the pros and the amateurs. With a professional he could read signs and intentions and probabilities. With an amateur anything could happen since triggers could be pulled, not always deliberately but because of impulses born of panic, or a simple spastic movement.

Aware of his intense and undivided attention as she took off the jersey she grimaced and said, dryly:

"Don't be embarrassed, snoop. I was a go-go for a while before I got sick of it, sometimes topless."

Fenner's grin was genuine as he remarked that he could see why. In sheer pantyhose her legs were long and straight and shapely, her midriff flat, the dark triangle defining her maturity faintly visible through the thin fabric.

She wore no bra and he mentally agreed she did not need one. Her young breasts, not large but rounded, were firm-looking and beautifully spaced.

When she caught him in an open-eyed stare at her near-nakedness she made a small face, her smirk more amused than lascivious. She was not flaunting her torso nor was she the least bit self-conscious; it was simply a part of her, like her ears. Fenner could feel the flush mounting in his cheeks but he still could not force his eyes away.

"Are they all right?" she said mischievously, confident of her appeal. "You've seen bigger ones, right? But in my kind of racket these work out better than the other kind. In the go-go bit they don't flop so much, you know? And in topless, when you're serving a guy lunch, you don't have to worry about the nipples dipping in his soup."

All this took no more than fifteen seconds and after the first proud pose she retrieved the short print dress he had heard described. She had it over her head a moment later and snatched up the gun as though still afraid that he might spoil things. This left her only one hand to tug at the dress, smoothing out the wrinkles at the bust and hips, the familiar feminine wiggle of those hips helping the operation.

The black dress, folded as neatly as she could manage with one hand, went into the case. The pumps, tucked inside with their plastic covers, were placed one at each end. She added the skirt and jersey; then as she started to lower the lid she thought of something else. As she straightened she caught her lower lip between her teeth and nibbled a moment, her young face tight with determination. It was then that Fenner spoke of something that had been bothering him all along.

"What I've been trying to understand," he said, "is, if you were where I think you were Saturday morning, why the hell you're still hanging around."

"How did you find me?" she asked, disdaining a reply.

Fenner waved one hand. "From my spies, informers, snitches," he said airily. Then, more seriously, "You were seen getting into a taxi. I know the driver. He told me where he dropped you."

Her disinterest in his reply surprised him and a moment later he saw the reason for her preoccupation. For she had leaned forward as he spoke and now she lifted one edge of the mattress. When he saw what she removed he understood that it had been secreted between mattress and box spring.

It was a brown Manila envelope about eleven-by-fourteen and bulky. As she placed it on top of the clothing and closed the suitcase something clicked in the back of his mind and he trapped the thought. Someone, he did not try to think who, had mentioned an envelope. Had someone stated that the dead man had carried such an envelope when noticed entering the building?

Aware that it would be futile to ask, he watched her lift the suitcase and back toward the door, retrieving her handbag as she did so. This presented a problem with the gun but she managed by slipping the strap up her arm and now Fenner swung his feet to the floor and sat up.

"You going to settle your bill?" he said as she put down the case and opened the door.

Her laugh was abrupt and humorless. "And give you a chance to tail me?"

"There's a law on the books about that. It's called defrauding an innkeeper. When I tell the owner you stiffed him he picks up the phone and every town cop and state policeman will be watching for your car. The registration card out front will have your plate number."

He wondered if she had even heard him until she said, "There's a good suit and a raincoat the guy can sell." She paused, the frown deepening. When she continued her voice was oddly wistful. "I guess you have to tell the police about me."

"I'd better if I want to keep my license."

"Yeah, well—thanks, Mr. Fenner. I mean for being decent about it. You know, not trying to jump me or anything and making me use this." She indicated the gun again and went on with some defiance. "But I still might take a pop at you if you stick your nose out before I get a start."

"Don't worry," Fenner said. "I only stick my nose out when I get paid for it."

She was gone then and Fenner rose, retrieved his wallet, and moved to the front window, hearing a car door open and slam. When the motor kicked over he opened the door far enough to see the small green two-door back from its slot. A green Plymouth, one of the economy models. It carried state plates and the sequence of letters and digits told him it was a rental car.

5

THE OWNER HIMSELF was behind the registration desk in the main unit, and when Fenner stated his request and backed it with both logic and sound reasoning, he became tractable if not enthusiastic in his cooperation.

His name was Harold Collins, a pot-bellied man in his fifties, with a slack, puffy face and stringy gray-blond hair; the disillusionment, deeply implanted in the pale blue eyes, was undisguised as he listened and shook his head.

"We're not allowed to give out that information," he said with quiet weariness.

Fenner had put his identification on the counter when he asked to see the registration form and now he slid a ten-dollar bill alongside it, smoothing it out with his fingertips.

"Think again, Mr. Collins," he said dryly. "You'll be asked the same thing by a couple of detectives later in the day and you'll answer them for free. Why not take a little profit? Because you sure as hell aren't going to take anything but a loss out of room sixteen."

"I'm not?" Collins did not touch the bill but his tone was that of a man who had just been gravely injured by a friend.

"The lady just packed and took off."

"But—I mean, I've got his credit card stamped and—"

"Signed?"

"Well, no. He said he might be here a couple of days and

wanted breakfast and I could fill in the amount when he checked out."

"The lady left you a suit and a raincoat to sell but you can't collect from a dead man. Now come on, let's have the registration."

Reaching now for the file box with some bewilderment, Collins selected a card. Not quite understanding until then, he turned back, eyes bulging and mouth atremble.

"Dead man?" he parroted. "What dead man?"

"Number sixteen. Did you see him this morning, or yesterday?"

As Collins stood in stunned silence, Fenner removed the card from fingers suffering from temporary paralysis. Turning it face up he took out a small notebook and reached for the desk pen.

Mr. & Mrs. Leslie Ludlow is what he read. A New York City address in the West Fifties, the number apparently not far from Eighth Avenue. The car registration number tallied with the one in his mind. He wrote it down and asked to see the credit card form. It was as Collins had said, stamped with the name and card number, but with amount due left blank.

Again Fenner asked his question and Collins, his mouth still agape, gulped and said, "What?"

"I asked if you'd seen Ludlow this morning or at any time yesterday."

Collins shook his head. "No," he said, drawing out the word; then, as though finally understanding the implication of Fenner's words, added, "Good God! He's not there now, is he? I mean you're not saying there's a body in unit sixteen?"

"No body. Alive or dead. No body at all. The woman just took off two or three minutes ago. The best you can do is fill in the amount on that credit card slip, send it in, and hope you get paid."

He handed back the registration card, thanked Collins for his cooperation. He repeated his earlier statement that the police would be dropping by later but assured him he had nothing to worry about.

As he turned away the man was still looking bewildered and traces of shock remained at the corners of his tired eyes. The ten lay untouched where Fenner had left it.

By delaying his return to his office so that he could stop at his apartment and do what he originally had in mind when he left Falmouth—how many hours ago was it?—Jack Fenner postponed some wear and tear on his emotions.

The shower had its expected therapeutic effect—hot, tepid, cool. The shave gave him a new face; fresh shorts and undershirt completed the feeling of cleanliness. Having hung up his badly wrinkled raincoat, he donned a pair of dark-brown double-knit slacks, white shirt, a maroon tie. The brown Shetland jacket, still unwrinkled by the nature of its weave, did not need changing.

As he turned off Boylston fifteen minutes later, he took the traffic citation from the glove compartment, perversely pleased now that he could have free parking for the rest of the day. He saw the white and blue squad car as he sought an empty space. It stood a few feet beyond the travel agency. When he noticed the unmarked police sedan close by, a curious sense of foreboding began to work on his imagination that was both perplexing and disturbing.

Seeking some explanation he wondered if the headquarters technical crew were still going over his office. Either that or—

Or what?

He parked hurriedly in the first available space and as he approached his building he understood the reason for the police car. For a uniformed officer now stood in the doorway, blocking it off. Pedestrians paused in their busy way for a peek or two but there was no congestion, no idle onlookers.

The policeman came to attention as Fenner angled in his direction. When he diagnosed Fenner's intention, he said:

"Only tenants allowed inside, Mister."

"I am a tenant. Fenner, third floor. What the hell's going on up there?"

"Fenner?" The cop squinted at him as though the name had some doubtful but magic quality. "You the one who has the office where they found the stiff this morning? . . . Okay, then. I guess the lieutenant will be wanting to see you."

"Lieutenant who?" Fenner said, unable yet to believe any of this.

"Bacon. Seems like they found another body up there. Maybe an hour ago. The morgue boys have already been here and gone but they're still working the office. Go ahead, Mr. Fenner."

Not bothering with the elevator, which had stopped at an upper floor, Fenner took the fire stairs two at a time and slid to a stop when he saw the second uniformed man outside the open door. It was then that the pressures of shock and new fear began to work on him and he had to force himself to keep moving.

That fear became at once real and sickening when he saw that it was not his office door that stood open but Fred Lipscomb's. It was here that the second officer stood, young and thickly sideburned, his gaze curious and challenging when Fenner stopped and peered beyond him. Apparently something in the grim, pale features, the hard-eyed look of shocked disbelief, kept the man silent until Fenner could force himself to speak.

"Tell the lieutenant Jack Fenner is out here," he said, understanding somehow what must have happened but unable and unwilling to accept such a frightful conclusion.

He half heard the officer speak to someone inside and then Bacon was there, a tight, strained expression on his bony face, the gray eyes angry and probing as he took Fenner's arm, guided him silently across the threshold and pulled him to a stop.

"This is far enough," he said bluntly. "You can't do any good in here and besides we're busy."

Fenner made no protest nor did he speak as his glance took in the outer office and the open doorway beyond. The experts were again busy going through the familiar routine, only now they had more to work with—the glass-topped tables, the glass showcases filled with stamps of all colors and designs but not the rare and valuable ones, Lipscomb had told him. A few hundred dollars' worth at best, the higher-priced items locked securely in the inner-office safe for those special customers who had money to spend.

The chalk outline on the carpet not far from where he stood served only to give added impetus to his mounting sense of loss and sadness; with it came a deep and punishing anger that had as its source a desire for revenge and retaliation.

Earlier that morning, in his office, the victim had been an unknown dead man, little different from others Fenner had seen as a police officer, faceless victims evoking no great sense of personal loss or unwanted emotion.

Leslie Ludlow—if that was his name—had been one of those. Finding him there in his, Fenner's, office and outraged that such a thing could happen to him, his basic reaction once his surprise had been conquered was nothing more than one of deep-seated resentment at whoever was responsible.

But Fred Lipscomb was a friend. Not a buddy-buddy friend; the age difference and a lack of common interests were too great for that. But a friend nonetheless, a harmless, gentlemanly, and aging man who bore no one ill-will. It was because of such thoughts that Fenner, needing some outlet for his bottled-up rage, began to curse—quietly, deliberately, savagely, and with great intensity. Not until he felt Bacon's grip tighten did he realize what he was doing or understand the lieutenant was speaking.

"What?" he said, forcing himself to concentrate.

"The son," Bacon said. "That's how we found him."

"The son?"

"The old man phoned him every Sunday. On Long Island where the son and wife and two kids live. Yesterday there was no phone call and no answer when the son tried to reach his father. He tried here and the apartment this morning and then grabbed the first flight out of La Guardia. The super here let him in the office and then called the precinct."

Fenner thought he understood it then even before Bacon showed him the two empty cartridge cases that had been found near the chalk marks.

"Same caliber as the others," he said. "Anything missing?"

"Not that we know of," Bacon said.

"No forced entry? Then Lipscomb must have heard the shots and stepped out into the hall—"

"Or was just leaving his office," Bacon finished. "Probably standing there when our killer came out of your office, maybe with the gun still in his hand."

Bacon continued his speculations in low vengeful tones but Fenner was no longer listening. He needed no help to visualize the scene and the specifics; the actual mechanics of the murder were unimportant.

"Shot close?" he asked finally.

"In the chest. The m.e. figures he died within minutes. If he'd stayed put, I mean Lipscomb, he'd probably be alive. But once the killer spotted him it was too late. A perfect witness; hadn't a chance then. Got backed in here at gunpoint and—"

He broke off, muttered something that sounded like "Goddamn murdering bastard"; then, just as suddenly, he was once again a veteran homicide cop, his mind on his job.

"Oh, yeah," he said, releasing Fenner's arm. "The son's name is Edward. He's waiting in your office. I had to get him out of here and your cleaning crew was just finishing and the place was open. You'll only be in the way here. So go on. He wants to talk to you anyway." He took a breath, expelled it noisily. "And so do I when we finish here."

Edward Lipscomb was sitting quietly in Alice Maxwell's chair when Jack Fenner entered his office. Taller than his father, soft-looking and perhaps thirty-five, he was getting quite bald in front and the brown eyes behind the dark-rimmed glasses were sick, the traces of shock and sadness still showing.

It had been a long time since Fenner faced a situation like this and he had trouble finding a way to express himself as he watched the other rise and tentatively offer his hand. It was a damp, hot handshake but when Lipscomb broke the silence, his voice was surprisingly steady.

"Hello, Mr. Fenner. I think we met about a year ago. Dad brought me in—"

"I remember."

"He was very fond of you. He spoke of you frequently."

"We were friends," Fenner said, wishing he had swallowed the thickness from the back of his throat before he spoke. To gain time he waved toward the inner office. "Let's sit in there. We'll have to wait for the lieutenant."

"I know."

They went in, Fenner sitting behind his desk and Lipscomb easing into a chair, an air of abstract bewilderment still evident in his softly modulated tones.

"I wanted him to get out of the city. Dad, I mean. I knew he'd never really retire or be happy living with us. But I thought a smaller town somewhere, maybe in Florida. Keep his hand in on a smaller scale, get rid of some of his inventory. Stamps weren't just a business with him you know; they were part of his life."

He paused, his gentle sad-looking eyes focused inward as he recounted other memories.

"We had a room for him at our house on Long Island but I knew he'd never use it while he could still get around. I did talk him into taking a trip to Florida last winter. I kept telling him how great it would be to have one of those small condominiums, maybe on the west coast around St. Petersburg or some quieter place farther down.

"I asked him about it when he got back. He said, yes, he'd looked at some condominiums, and some were pretty nice. He'd brought back some literature and price lists and floor plans. He said someday maybe, but he wasn't quite ready for that sort of living yet. . . ."

His voice trailed off and Fenner watched miserably, not knowing any way to express further sympathy, but realizing that it would be better to change the subject and get the man's mind off the past.

"I guess you know what happened here earlier," he said finally. "This is where it started. Right out there in that office. Some poor bastard I'd never seen before."

"Oh, yes. The lieutenant explained things. I'm sure he's right; there's no other answer, is there? Dad was just unlucky." He sat up, a new determination showing now. It was at once evident in the hardening of his tone, some undercurrent of vindictiveness in the cadence of his voice. "But someone is going to pay. Will you help me, Mr. Fenner? Dad spoke highly of you. He said you were expensive but the best in the business."

The unexpected proposition threw Fenner off balance. He wasn't ready for it and the flat green eyes reflected that uncertainty. In that moment of indecision he found himself fumbling for words.

"But the police—"

"Oh, I know they'll do their best. I don't expect any miracles from you; just your help. I have to do everything I can even if it seems childish and futile to you. I mean, if you came up with just one solid bit of evidence or proof that would help—and who can say you won't?—it will be worthwhile."

He lifted one hand to forestall a premature reply. "My father was not a wealthy man but when his attorney and the tax people inventory his safe I know there will be a sizeable estate. Dad hinted as much. So I'm going to spend some of it with you. Will you do what you can? For him—and me?"

He already had his checkbook out, his attitude that of one whose offer has just been accepted. "Do you work by the day?"

Fenner, at the point of refusing the offer, had a sudden change of mind when his brain finally began to function in its customary sound and practical manner. His decision, when he made it, was based on simple common sense.

"I was going to say no," he began, "because I'm just as much interested in catching this killer as you are. I was going to give it all I had even if I struck out. But in my business a paying client is almost a must. Without one I have to pretty much level with the police. Withholding information can not only cost me my license but get me in a jam. But a certain confidential relationship exists between an investigator and his client. I have a moral obligation to protect that client's privacy and rights—within reason. It gives me a reason to dig legitimately into things that I otherwise might have to pass up. Also I've got an additional motive—to earn my fee.

"So all right, Mr. Lipscomb. No miracles but I've been known to get lucky. And no, I don't work by the day. Hourly. Twenty bucks. Because it's fairer. I work on several things most of the time. Maybe two hours for you in one stretch; five in another. For any number of reasons I may have to knock off temporarily on a job before I can get back to it again. Your hours will be accounted for."

He was watching Lipscomb writing a check as he spoke and when he accepted it he saw it was made out for five hundred dollars.

"Here's for the first twenty-five hours. There'll be plenty more where that comes—"

He got that far when the outer door opened and Lieutenant Bacon entered, Sergeant Gaynor at his heels. This time Bacon got right to the point, a working cop again now that the time for sympathy was past.

"We're about finished in there, Mr. Lipscomb," he said. "Do you have an attorney in town?"

"I'm using my father's. He said he'd wait for me in his office. He has a key, also the combination to the safe."

Bacon watched Lipscomb rise. "You'll be in town a while?"

"At the Parker House. For at least two or three days."

Bacon said fine and Lipscomb said he had hired Fenner to help out and he hoped Bacon wouldn't mind.

6

LIEUTENANT BACON SETTLED his lanky frame in a chair when the outer door closed and motioned Sergeant Gaynor to do the same. For the next few seconds he looked at Fenner, saying nothing, and Fenner returned the stare with steady eyes, content to let Bacon have the first conversational serve. Presently it came.

"All right." Bacon cleared his throat. "Where've you been the past couple of hours?"

"Here and there."

"Doing what?"

"Helping you do your job."

Bacon bristled visibly, ready to take offense where none was meant. "What's that crack supposed to mean?"

"No crack," Fenner said mildly. "I told you I'd be digging around. I did. Have you identified the first guy yet?"

"If we haven't—I haven't checked lately—we will. Why? You think you've got a lead?"

"I think I've got more than that." Fenner looked at Gaynor. "Got your notebook, Joe?"

When he had consulted his own little book he said, "I think the guy's name was Leslie Ludlow," and went on to give the New York City address he had noted.

He spoke evenly, not bragging, just stating a fact. For a

moment then Bacon simply stared in open-mouthed amazement.

"I'll be a sonofabitch," he said, and then, almost predictably, doubt narrowed his gray gaze. For he was jealous of his prerogatives and unaccustomed to such informative windfalls. "What tipped you? You were alone with that body. If you found something on him, if you've been holding out on us—"

He was beginning to sputter and get red in the face and Gaynor spoke sharply, forestalling a possible stroke.

"Lieutenant!"

It was enough to get attention.

"How about letting Jack tell it?"

Bacon thought about it and had the grace to show embarrassment. "Sure."

"I found nothing that you didn't see," Fenner said, annoyed by the accusation but understanding the reason for it. "I talked to some of the neighborhood people and I got lucky. Now, do you want to hear it or shall I save it for the D.A.?"

For two seconds Bacon considered the challenge. He shifted his rear end in the chair and studied Gaynor without rancor. When he gave in he did so reluctantly but without resentment.

"Okay. Just give us all of it. From the top."

Fenner did so. He spoke of those he had questioned and the break he got from Lonny Parks. Bacon listened intently, not interrupting and eyes full of thought. Not until Fenner told how he had been surprised by the woman in the motel room did he ask a question.

"You didn't want to go up against the gun, hunh? Figure she'd use it?"

"She was smart enough not to let me get within five feet of it and I wasn't about to jump her. When I go up against a gun these days I want to be paid for it. Just like you do."

Bacon nodded. He was thinking like the veteran officer he was now and when Fenner mentioned the information he obtained from the motel owner, Bacon hiked his chair closer to the desk and reached for the telephone. As he dialed he asked Fenner to repeat the car's license number.

"Sam?" he said when he had his connection. "Lieutenant Bacon. Check a registration for me, will you?" He repeated the number, adding, "I think it's a rental car."

While he waited he asked Fenner for the telephone directory, motioning that it should be passed to Gaynor. He leaned back, eyes inspecting the molding on the ceiling, lost in his private thoughts.

"Yeah, Sam," he said finally. "Right. Yeah . . . Thanks." He hung up and addressed Gaynor. "Thrift Cars," he said. "Give me a number."

Gaynor did so and Bacon dialed, identified himself, and asked his questions. There were several of these and when he hung up it was apparent that the answers had been satisfactory.

"Well, you were right," he said. "On all counts. Rented Friday afternoon. The name on the credit card was Leslie Ludlow. But get this. About an hour ago a woman called and said she couldn't return the car but they could pick it up on Charles Street. They did. Already had a traffic ticket on it."

He pushed the telephone away. "So what have we got? Saul Klinger and the hackie put this Mrs. Ludlow, or whatever her name is, on the scene Saturday morning at about the right time. To get here she either rode in with Ludlow—and if she did why would she take a cab back to the motel?"

"Or she followed him in, using a cab and knowing where he was going," Fenner added.

"And if she killed Ludlow or knew he was dead she could have panicked and grabbed a cab because she was afraid to drive the rental." Bacon weighed these possibilities before he added, "Well, she has no car now. To get out of town she has to use a bus, train, plane—or hitchhike."

He stood up, asking Fenner to give Gaynor a full description of the woman and pacing impatiently while this was being done.

"I'll call New York when I get back to the office," he said half to himself. "They can stake out the Ludlow address in case she shows. Meanwhile, we'll get out a city APB and a six-state bulletin and keep our fingers crossed."

Gaynor coughed. When Bacon turned to give him a questioning glance he said, "She hasn't got a car now, Lieutenant. I mean, the all-points won't help much."

"That's right, she hasn't," Bacon's glance was approving as he considered his sergeant. "But she's got a credit card, right? If she's real cute she might try to get another wagon from Avis or Hertz or National. But you're right about the APB for now. Use that phone out there." He pointed to Fenner's anteroom.

"Get the description to the headquarters dispatcher. I want the bus stations, Back Bay, South Station, Logan International covered. Also the hotels for recent registrations. Avis and Hertz and National like I said. *If* she picks up another car before those offices get the word, then we put out the bulletin."

Bacon sat down again and presently Fenner could hear Gaynor on the other telephone. For perhaps a minute Bacon sat unmoving, distance in his unfocused gaze. When he finally spoke his voice was low-keyed and traces of concern showed in the corners of his eyes.

"I guess this one got to you some," he said.

"If you mean Lipscomb, one hell of a lot more than some. This thing here is one big pain in the ass and I sure as hell want to know who picked my office for a shooting gallery. But Lipscomb—"

His voice thickened and he stopped. Bacon said, "Sure," and stood up.

It was then that a remembered phrase came back to Fenner. It was nothing spoken and he could not recall in what context his brain had fashioned it. But at some point he had told himself in great resentment and disgust that his office had been used as a meeting place for murder. He was determined now to do all he could to prove to the killer that his anteroom was in fact no place for murder.

But he said none of this to Bacon as he watched him join Gaynor. When the pair left the outer office he began to review the things he had told Bacon and only then did he admit to a small twinge of guilt that he tried to justify. In the beginning his failure to mention the fat Manila envelope was not deliberate. His mind occupied with relating an accurate account of his movements, he did not even remember that one detail until Bacon was ready to leave. He didn't attempt to excuse the oversight because it would not hinder the search for the woman. But the thought of the envelope reminded him of something else, and he now brought forth the crumpled sheet that had remained in his jacket pocket ever since he jammed it there so hurriedly when the motel door opened, trapping him.

Whether or not this carbon copy with its cryptic columns of letters and figures would prove to be a vital piece of evidence did not seem important. Bacon had enough to do following accepted procedures, but his own curiosity had to be satisfied and now he flattened the sheet on his desk and tried to press out the wrinkles.

In that first and only instant of inspection back at the motel the contents meant nothing to him. Now he saw that the right-hand column was a simple list of figures. The initials on the left continued to puzzle him until he retrieved from the cobwebs of his mind the suspicion that at least three of those letter combinations seemed vaguely familiar. He did not know why or in what context.

But he sensed that he was close to some sort of answer and he looked away, gaze fixed sightlessly out the window, his brows all humps and wrinkles as he tried to concentrate. Presently he began to repeat the letters aloud, slowly, his enunciation deliberate, analyzing the sounds as he sought some term of reference until, like some brilliant idea whose time has come for fulfillment, his area of speculation narrowed, focused, and was at last acceptable.

His smile came automatically and he spoke without knowing it in this moment of self-congratulation. "Hell, yes," he said. "It almost has to be." And now his fingertip isolated and pounced on one of the symbols on the list in front of him, a two-letter combination.

EK

No punctuation, just the two capitals. And to a broker, a stock trader, a tape watcher, EK stood for Eastman Kodak.

In his modest stock portfolio acquired over several years were shares of that stock which had split and multiplied most profitably and it was one of the few ticker symbols he was able to recognize. Now as his eye moved laterally to the opposite number—800—he tried to recall the last market quotation he had noticed. Somewhere around 90? That times 800 would represent $72,000.

For many minutes then he sat where he was, testing and rejecting assumptions. He related these to things that had happened that morning, the relative possibilities, the reason for such a list, the original of which may have been on Leslie Ludlow's person at the time of his murder. In the end he reached for the telephone and dialed the number of Carter & Townsend.

To the female voice that answered he said, "Mr. Townsend. Alan Townsend." When the next voice said, "Mr. Townsend's office," he said, "Is he in? This is Mr. Fenner."

After a slight delay Alan Townsend came on. "Yes, Jack."

"I have to see you," Fenner said, wasting no time on the amenities. "Can you give me a few minutes? I could stop in after the market closes if you're busy now. It's pretty important or I wouldn't ask."

There followed a moment of silence; then, "Well, sure. I guess so. But if it's about some investment of yours—"

"It isn't," Fenner said flatly. "I need a little help on something. I'll try to keep it short."

"Sure, Jack. Four o'clock will be fine. In my office."

When Fenner hung up he carefully refolded the carbon

copy, slipped it back into his inside pocket, and removed his jacket. With a half-formed idea already taking root in his brain, he stood and moved over to the steel filing cabinet. Because most of the drawers contained carbon copies of confidential reports he had the only key and when he had unlocked the cabinet he bent over to slide out the bottom drawer.

Because Alice Maxwell knew about its contents and purpose she had given it a name—the odds-and-ends drawer, an appropriate enough term considering its purpose.

Inside were perhaps thirty or forty file folders of varying bulk. They contained a motley collection of clippings which Fenner had found interesting and to which he added from time to time, their source local newspapers, press association stories, columnists' pieces along with items from such magazines as *Time*. Fenner's filing system was his own and every year or so he would take an afternoon off to discard stories that either were no longer of interest to him or had outlived their usefulness. Although seldom consulted, there were occasions when a filed piece of information had proved most helpful. To have such a file at hand also saved him trips to the public library that might otherwise have been necessary.

For although most of Fenner's work these days came from three or four prominent legal firms, an occasional assignment was offbeat and required some specialized knowledge with which he was not familiar. It was in such instances that the file had proved valuable and right now he knew exactly which folder he wanted.

It dealt with the near-scandalous series of thefts from prominent banks and brokers that had started two or three years back and, according to those stories he remembered, provided enormous sums of illicit funds for the mob members. Stock certificates, bonds, Treasury notes—all useful if not entirely negotiable. What made him think of this folder now was a clipping Alice had pointed out, a newsworthy theft that had taken place less than three weeks earlier. He picked this item first, once he had spread out the clippings. He read the lead paragraph.

It was a wire service story datelined New York City and printed locally. It read:

One of the largest holdups of the year took place yesterday morning when a messenger for Clyde & Company was held up by two armed men, forced at gunpoint into an alley off Spring Street, and relieved of stock certificates valued at $3.8 million. Thought to be mob-inspired, this latest theft is the largest since $15.3 million in negotiable Treasury bills vanished from a locked and guarded room at the headquarters of the First Manhattan Bank more than a year ago. Neither New York City detectives nor the FBI have a clue as yet but the investigation is continuing.

Fenner read the whole article, put it aside on one corner of his desk, and began to scan the remaining clippings. The first to claim his attention was another piece, this one from *Time* and published about the time of the First Manhattan job. He paid particular attention to certain paragraphs, the first of which was a statement from some expert who said:

"The total take is enormous. J. Henry Wallace, the chairman of a firm that keeps track of missing securities, estimates that $50 billion in illegitimate paper is afloat, most of it in blue-chip stocks and some of it federal, state, municipal and corporate bonds. Insurance companies are the ultimate victims. They must make good to an insured bank or brokerage house that takes a loss by theft or by buying hot securities in good faith."

Farther along he saw a quote from a Senate investigation subcommittee witness, who stated in part:

"We got to a point where we put orders in. You know, specific issues in specific denominations. Like some high school kid will come along, and he works for eight or nine years with a clean record, gets promoted a couple of times and then gets hooked up with the wrong guy or girl.

"Brokerage firm employees who gamble, or who are in the hands of the 'shylocks' are especially attractive. You could never operate or even begin if you didn't have crooked bankers, crooked C.P.A.s, crooked brokers."

The final paragraph, not a quote, stated:

The mobsters often sell the hot securities at a discount, netting ten to fifteen percent for the hot certificates to fifty percent or more for cold, or clean, stock that has been switched by some clerk or minor official and goes unreported as stolen for months or even years. Sometimes the mobsters use the securities as collateral for personal loans. Too many U.S. banks, eager for business, accept these securities without checking their validity. Foreign bankers are often just as careless. . . .

And still a third clip caught Fenner's eye. This one, also dated many months earlier, had been written by a nationally syndicated Washington columnist, who wrote:

The bogus stocks and bonds are also used by organized crime to build and renovate villas and condominiums along the Costa del Sol in Spain and the Algarve on Portugal's southern coast.

The alarming new element in this ocean of fraudulent paper, aside from increased volume, is that banks around the world are being used more and more to generate solid cash from bad securities. . . .

"The Swiss are up to their necks in it," one frustrated federal investigator told us. "Dubious bank deals have also been found in Belgium, Holland, Hong Kong, Lebanon, Panama, Luxembourg. . . ."

Finally, from the same article, Fenner read:

But now far more sophisticated techniques are used to escape detection. In one common hustle, the Mafia sells the hot certificates for cash to a failing company. The failing company does not sell the certificates for cash, which would be risky. Instead, it simply puts the certificates in its safe. There the unwitting accounting firm verifies the existence of the securities and duly approves the company's books. Such securities are listed as assets, enabling the firm to borrow money from a bank.

If the company manages not to fail, no one is the wiser. If it does fail, the banks are usually protected by insurance, so they have no compelling reason to inquire into the integrity of the paper that has shored up the failing company. . . .

When Fenner finished his research, he tried to think not only logically but sensibly. Usually in his investigations, of whatever nature, he had an orderly, often preconceived line of procedure, the problem the simple one of how to get what he wanted. In this instance he felt no such confidence. And since he had no acceptable or even workable hypothesis, he had to use what was available, collect all the information he could, even if seemingly irrelevant, and hope it might prove productive. For this reason he sought and quickly found another source of possible information.

A glance at his watch told him there was very little time left to keep his appointment with Alan Townsend, but he still had one call to make and he mentally phrased his verbal approach as he replaced the file and locked the cabinet.

He kept his fingers crossed as he dialed. His luck was still holding and Kent Murdock answered.

"I need another favor," he began, coming right to the point.

"Another one?" Murdock's tone was at once wary. "Did you see the afternoon edition yet? Well, the scene of the crime this morning remains unidentified. So what's the favor? You want your picture taken?"

Fenner laughed to show he appreciated the crack. He thanked Murdock for keeping his name out of the paper and said, "What's your financial editor's name? I don't think I've met him."

"Fred Sampson."

"Is he approachable? What kind of office hours does he keep?"

"Banker's. Nine-thirty, when he feels like it, to five or so. Why?"

"I want to pick his brains. I've got to run, but would you do this? Call him and tell him I'll stop in his office around five or before. You don't have to call back. If he'll see me, fine; if not

I'll only have wasted a trip and I can hit him in the morning. Tell him I'll buy the drinks or dinner if he can spare the time."

"I'll tell him," Murdock said. And then, with some suspicion, "Has this got anything to do with those killings? Because if it has, and you get an angle—"

"I know, I know," Fenner cut in. "After Lieutenant Bacon you'll be the first to know. Already I owe you. Start dreaming about how I can pay off, okay?"

7

THE FIRM of Carter & Townsend had moved from the original two-story stone building designed with the solid impressiveness of many banks of that day. For the past five years they had occupied the first two floors of a more modern office building, but much of the furniture had also made the move, particularly the three rows of chairs for tape watchers important enough to justify the space. The chairs were mahogany, with arms and rounded backs, padded there and on the seat with black leather, and the regular viewers seemed evenly divided between the active daily traders and the esteemed and affluent elderly customers who wished for the most part to idle away an hour or two a day.

On the right, extending toward the rear, were six or seven plain wooden desks for the customer's men, each with telephones and a Telequote desk unit where the current bid-and-ask quotes appeared on a screen when the proper buttons were pushed with the symbol assigned to that particular stock.

At this hour only two of these desks were occupied—Fenner's man had apparently left for the day—and the two young employees, one with longish hair and one more modish, were on the telephone. The Translux tape was already dark, the customers' chairs vacant. Three young women, clerks or secretaries, moved here and there with businesslike efficiency but with no discernible purpose.

Jack Fenner, pausing for a moment just inside the massive doors, glanced at the private offices which took up most of the right-hand wall. The largest, at the far end, was the sanctuary of Jonathan Carter, son of one of the original partners, in his late sixties now and largely inactive. Adjacent was the office of his son-in-law, a tall, proper man named Addison with whom Fenner had no more than a nodding acquaintance. The middle office, untenanted, was used for a conference room; that left the first two offices for the Townsend brothers, since their father, Paton Townsend, a man of Jonathan Carter's generation, was a semi-invalid and confined to the family home within reach of a respirator to combat what was said to be a terminal case of emphysema.

The office on Fenner's immediate right, the first in line, belonged to Alan Townsend not only because he was the most dependable and accessible partner but because he was the hardest working and most capable. Now, seeing no one he knew, and ignored by those who were still busy, Fenner knocked at Townsend's door and once again he considered his approach and sought the appropriate phrases with which to make his request sound reasonable enough to get the cooperation he desired.

Not sure whether he heard an invitation to enter, he opened the door far enough to poke his head inside, waiting until he saw Townsend's small automatic smile and nod of recognition. Closing the door behind him he noticed that the adjacent small office of Townsend's private secretary was empty so he advanced, impressed once more, not by the size of the office but by the quality and good taste of the furnishings which seemed also to have been moved intact from the original founders' building.

By then Townsend was on his feet, and because Fenner was an infrequent visitor—last Thursday was an exception—he offered his hand and motioned Fenner to a nearby chair before seating himself.

"Well, how was the weekend?" he asked pleasantly. "I hope you did better with your Saturday golf at Woods Hole than I did."

"Financially, yes," Fenner said, and took a moment to consider this man and his background.

Proper was the word that came first to mind, a throwback somehow to what was sometimes called a gentleman of the old school. He had a trim, compact body, not big—perhaps five-ten and a hundred and sixty pounds—but fit-looking. His hair was black and straight and cut short, yet long enough to part. His eyes, like his hair, were dark and intelligent and Fenner had never seen him, at least in the office, looking anything but immaculate, his well-tailored suits invariably either blue or some acceptable shade of gray; always a white shirt, his neckties either plain-colored or conservatively striped. No one had ever characterized him as a "fun person" but for all of that he was a likable man, his manner of speaking cultivated but not stiff.

Even his divorce had been handled without scandal or publicity, thanks in part to the way Fenner had gathered the necessary and irrefutable evidence. For the one exception to Townsend's basic conservatism had come when he made the mistake of marrying an empty-headed piece of fluff whose masquerade during courtship apparently blinded him emotionally, a pretty young woman with the proper antecedents and connections, a society type who had the body and inclination for more excitement and sexual variety than her husband could, or would, provide.

"So what can I do for you, Jack?" he asked politely. "I believe you said it was not an investment matter."

Fenner, who had remained standing, unfolded his carbon and placed it the right way up for Townsend to examine.

"I lied a little. It has to do with investments but not the way you mean. Information is what I need, and maybe an opinion. I could probably do it myself if I had one of those pocket calculators but—well, take a look."

Townsend, who had been doing just that as Fenner spoke, looked up, his smile quizzical and mildly speculative. Not normally given to profanity in any context, he indulged himself, his tone impressed.

"This"—he dropped the sheet—"is a hell of a portfolio. Don't tell me you've been accumulating a secret account with some other broker?"

"No way." Fenner chuckled and sat down. "I only wish I had one like it. No," he added soberly, "what I want, if you can spare the time, is for you to identify the individual stocks from that column of symbols—I only recognize the EK and the TX—and estimate the value of the list."

Townsend started to reply, his expression suggesting compliance; then, with a broker's acquired caution, he let one eyelid droop.

"Would you want to tell me why you feel it's important?"

"If you'll supply the information, yes. Absolutely."

"Fair enough." Townsend picked up a desk pen. "All right to figure on this sheet?"

"If you'll keep it neat, I'll want photocopies. I'd like the stock name beside the symbol; the total worth next to the number of shares."

Townsend leaned forward only to ask a final question. "Do you have to have today's closing quotes?"

"No. Friday's prices will do."

"Fine." Townsend reached for that week's *Barron's*, which had been discarded in his wastebasket. Flipping back to the proper pages, he said, "Now let's see—"

He got that far when the door was flung open and Bruce Townsend rushed in in his characteristic headlong fashion.

"Hey, Alan!" he began, and stopped when he saw Fenner. "Hi, Jack." Then, surprised but not apologetic, he repeated the word. "Hey, you guys busy?"

"Sort of," Alan said. "But come in, we can use some help."

"Well—" Bruce Townsend frowned uncertainly. "I called Laura and told her if she'd stop by I'd give her a lift. Is it going to take long?"

"Not if you sit down and pitch in. Jack wants an estimate on this portfolio." He offered the sheet. "Take a look."

Bruce scanned the list. When he returned it he grinned approvingly.

"I like it," he said, nodding. "Whose is it?"

"Jack hasn't said. Pull up a chair." Alan pushed the open *Barron's* to one end of the desk. "I'll give you the stock from the symbols and you jot down the closing quotes."

Bruce did as directed and as they began to call out the individual stocks and prices Fenner leaned back and gave his attention to the younger Townsend.

Five years or so Alan's junior, it was at once apparent that Bruce Townsend came as close to being the exact opposite of his brother as one could imagine. There was one good genetic reason for this as Fenner knew—they had been conceived and borne by different mothers. There had also been a third Mrs. Paton Townsend some years later and again a single heir, this one a girl, much younger and presently in Florence, Italy, studying art or going to art school; Fenner could not recall which.

Now, musing about the obvious contrast in the brothers, Fenner reviewed the things he had heard about Bruce Townsend's recent past. Unlike the trim, dark, and proper Alan, Bruce was taller, broader, and more obviously physical. Instead of a business suit he wore slacks and an expensive jacket of gray herringbone. His medium-blond hair, sun-bleached at the edges, was thick and wavy, full-cut now but without extended sideburns. He had been a good athlete in prep school and at Harvard, a minor hero who traded on good looks, an easy charm, and an outgoing personality. Unpredict-able and caring little for the conventions, he had left a lovely and devoted wife some months earlier to move into his club, at the same time providing a small apartment for the woman he had just mentioned—Laura Latimer, a former model and would-be actress from New York. In addition he had managed to find her a suitable job in the public-relations department of a nearby advertising agency.

Even so there had been no divorce in spite of the obvious grounds for action and Bruce's willingness to make it uncontested, although Fenner had heard that lawyers had been consulted. Old Paton Townsend, probably the happiest man at the wedding in his assumption that he was getting the finest woman in the world as a daughter-in-law, and now confined to his home as a physical cripple, could only rage and damn his errant son. Threats of disinheritance unless the present affair was promptly terminated before it was too late proved ineffective, since there was a trust fund established by Bruce's mother that would eventually be his. . . .

Some movement pulled Fenner's thoughts back from his mind-wandering musing and he saw that Bruce Townsend was moving toward the door.

"Finished?" he asked, eyeing Alan with some surprise.

"Shortly," Townsend said. "He's gone to get a desk calculator."

When Bruce came back and placed the electronic unit near his brother's right hand, Alan said, "The rest of it's easy if you want to run."

"I told you I had to wait for Laura." Bruce looked at Fenner, a touch of approval in his engaging smile. "Some portfolio," he said. "Almost half growth—and I don't mean those hot over-the-counter issues that are always going to be another Xerox or I.B.M.—Eastman, DuPont, Pfizer, Minnesota Mining—stocks like that. The cyclicals—oils, steels, metals; a couple of inbetweeners like Inland and Raytheon—many selling at six or seven times earnings or less. Where'd you get it anyway?"

Fenner was saved a reply by a tap on the door, which then opened cautiously, and Laura Latimer eased into the room like a person unaware of her welcome and ready with an apology for the intrusion. Her quick dark glance hesitated only a moment on Fenner before resting on Bruce, who at once stepped toward her.

"I peeked in your office, first," she began, offering him a cheek to kiss as he slipped one arm lovingly around her slim waist. "If you're busy . . ." she added, knowing quite well the remark was unnecessary and accepting the quick denial.

"Just about finished," Bruce said, drawing her toward a chair. "A couple of minutes."

Fenner, sneaking a look as she was being attended to, was again aware of the woman's obvious physical appeal. He had seen the two of them together several times during the past few months at restaurants and cocktail lounges but only once had he actually met her. They had accidentally rubbed elbows at the small Ritz bar, and Bruce had introduced her proudly and without embarrassment even though he knew Fenner was aware of his marital infidelity.

She had been pleasant enough then, her interest in Bruce apparently genuine. A slight Southern accent that Fenner could not place, as well as her dark attractiveness, had intrigued him, and he had asked what part of the South she was from.

"What they call a border state, actually," she had said.

"Tennessee?" he said, guessing.

"Kentucky. I thought I'd pretty well outgrown it."

"Actors' school in New York," Bruce had explained. "She's been working on all kinds of accents—I mean she did until she moved up here—part of her training."

Now in a simple tailored dress that did nice things for her supple, well-formed figure, Fenner noted again the smooth olive skin, the strong brows, the straight classic nose. The sharp, clean features gave her somehow a Castilian look that was oddly appealing. Unadorned except for a modest string of pearls and a large diamond solitaire on the proper finger— Fenner guessed the stone was a good three carats—her face was also devoid of makeup except where lipstick had been skillfully applied to make more generous and inviting the small, determined mouth. To complete the attempt to achieve individuality she wore her shining black hair parted and pulled back into a neat bun at the nape. The effect was severe but on her it looked good. . . .

Aware that someone had spoken, he yanked his thoughts back in time to realize that Alan Townsend had addressed him.

"Sorry."

Bruce Townsend said, "Alan says are you ready for the total? You want it exact?"

Fenner chuckled to cover his confusion. "Make it to the nearest thousand."

"As of Friday night's close," Alan said, "four hundred and one thousand." He pushed the completed list to the center of the desk and leaned back in his chair, relaxing. "Now it's your turn," he announced, his tone challenging. "Whose portfolio is it, where did you get it, what makes it important?"

Fenner stood and moved to pick up the sheet, not really surprised at the figure but impressed. He knew he owed them an explanation and considered the proper way to make it. To gain time he offered an apologetic smile and asked if it was possible to get three or four photocopies.

"I'll want to keep this," he added to justify his request, "and I'll have to give a copy to Lieutenant Bacon down at homicide in the morning."

That got instant attention but the quick reactions varied.

"Who the hell's Lieutenant Bacon?" Bruce asked.

"Homicide?" Alan's brows jerked upward.

"Wait a minute." This was Laura. "What's this all about anyway?"

As expected Alan Townsend was the first to regain his poise. He said certainly they could make copies and turned to his brother. By this time the woman was on her feet.

"Let me," she said. "I do that sort of thing all the time. Where's your copier?"

Bruce told her and she started out only to stop at the door and caution them. "Just hold that explanation until I get back, you hear?"

Fenner got a cigarette going and when the silence became uncomfortable he asked if he should wait until Laura Latimer returned. Bruce said she wasn't going to like it if Fenner didn't. Then she came back with the original and three copies and Fenner said:

"I don't know whose portfolio it is or exactly what it means. But I can tell you where I got that carbon. . . . Have any of you seen an afternoon paper? . . . Well, when you do, if you look carefully you'll probably find a couple of paragraphs about an unidentified man shot twice in the back of the head in a downtown office. That office was mine," he added, and went on to give a quick, expurgated account, telling no more than he had to and ignoring interruptions which soon stopped as the interest of his audience grew and a certain air of suspense kept them silent. He was also particularly careful to make no mention of the bulky envelope that the woman who may have been Mrs. Leslie Ludlow had removed from the motel mattress.

All three seemed impressed when he finished—Bruce frowning, Laura motionless and unwavering in her attention, and Alan grave but no emotion showing. As the senior officer present and probably the most intelligent, he was the first to speak.

"This carbon was in the victim's extra suit hanging in the motel room. How do you interpret that?"

"I don't."

"You must have some idea."

"If you want an assumption I'll give you one," Fenner said. "I'd guess that the original of that list was on him when he was shot. His pockets were stripped. The only inference I can make is that he may also have had the stock certificates represented by that list. No stock certificates have been found, at least not by me."

"And whoever killed him took them?" Bruce said hesitantly.
"Probably."

"And is that list going to help you any?" Laura Latimer
asked, her tone polite but full of doubt. "It sounds to me as if
you wanted to find the killer because you're sore at him for
picking your office to do his killing in."

Fenner had no objection to such reasoning but something
about the cool appraisal nettled him.

"There's a little more to it than that now," he said with a
touch of annoyance, and went on to speak of Fred Lipscomb's
brutal murder and its obvious explanation. "Whoever did the
killing was either a sociopath—a hired hand without any
capacity for conscience or guilt feelings—or a scared and
desperate individual who deliberately planned the first job and
was panicked into the second one.

"However it happened," he added, "his son hired me this
morning to do whatever I can to help the police investigation.
A long shot, right? I told him so. But you're right about one
thing: this is kind of personal now and sometimes a guy gets
lucky.

"Up to now all I have is this." He folded the copies with
care and slipped them into a side pocket. "But I have to start
somewhere and my hunch says this, or what it represents,
could be a motive."

Because he wanted to get away he pretended the subject
was closed; his tight, angular face and the cold flat look in his
green eyes said so. This was really not difficult to do because
all three had the subdued, impressed manner of any group
whose minds remained on an unfamiliar subject—a double
murder.

"But you'll let us know?" Alan said as Fenner reached for
the doorknob.

Fenner said they could count on it, and spoke again of his
appreciation for their help and cooperation.

8

FRED SAMPSON, the financial editor of the *Courier,* was a slight, untidy, bookish-looking man with wispy graying hair and thick-rimmed glasses with wide sidebows. He could have been fifty, and sitting down it was hard to tell how tall he was, but Jack Fenner was certain he could not have weighed more than a hundred and thirty pounds.

The office that Fenner entered after a polite knock was hardly more than a cubbyhole, with one dusty window and an ancient desk littered with papers and stacks of folders and reports, some of them a foot high. In addition to the chair the editor occupied, there was a straight-back chair tight up against one end of the desk, a metal typewriter stand at the other. The machine was an electric, the only new-looking object in the room. The rickety bookcase had four shelves which held some weighty reference volumes, countless magazines, and still more file folders.

Sampson nodded when Fenner introduced himself but did not rise or offer to shake hands, which were clasped behind his neck as he leaned back to inspect his visitor, his look at once appraising and somewhat skeptical. Aware finally that Fenner was looking for some place to sit, he picked up still more folders from the chair and deposited them on the floor.

"Sit down," he said.

Fenner, not sure how to take the casual reception, sat and said he hoped he wasn't holding Sampson up. The editor said he was usually here until six or so but offered no encouragement. The straight-stemmed briar he had clamped in one corner of his mouth was either out or empty and he spoke past it.

"Murdock wasn't sure just what it was you wanted from me. Something about a murder. In your office, wasn't it?"

Fenner kept his explanation as short as he could, at the same time unfolding his photocopies and passing one to Sampson, who had to sit up to receive it. In the hope that he could generate at least a bit of interest from the still uninterested editor, Fenner said:

"What's your opinion of that?"

Sampson removed the pipe and examined the sheet. When he was ready he said, "I like it. Yours?"

"Hardly." Fenner smiled to indicate his appreciation of Sampson's humor. "It's a copy of a sheet found among the victim's effects."

"Just like it is? Amounts and everything?"

"No amounts. Just the symbols and figures. I've a small account with Carter and Townsend. The Townsend brothers supplied the totals from today's *Barron's*. I just came from there."

Sampson nodded and returned the copy. He looked at his pipe and seemed surprised to find it empty. As he began to paw over the litter on his desk, apparently in search of tobacco, Fenner was aware of a growing sense of discouragement as the silence continued. He had several questions in mind that needed answers and he knew somehow that he had to get the man's interest.

Fred Sampson wrote a daily investment column which, although he had been unable to syndicate it, was very popular locally. It was a question-and-answer sort of column and had earned a faithful and loyal readership. Since Fenner was one of Sampson's readers, he considered saying how much he liked

what Sampson wrote until he realized that it might sound too
ordinary or too gratuitously flattering.

Then, even as he discarded the thought, common sense
came to his aid. For he had learned long ago that one way to
stimulate cooperation was to talk a man's language, to prove
that one had at least some knowledge, even if superficial, of
the other's field. He began by speaking of his own file of
clippings, quoting some of them having to do with the rash
of security thefts, many Mafia inspired, which had begun two
or three years earlier.

"One report I read," he said, "stated that the losses could
exceed fifty billion."

Perking up slightly as he filled his pipe, Sampson nodded his
agreement.

"Probably true."

"But my reports said a lot of those losses were never even
reported to the city police or the F.B.I."

"Also true."

"Why?"

"Image mostly."

"Image?"

Sampson pointed the stem of his unlit pipe. "A report of loss
to the authorities means the newspapers are going to print it.
How does it look when you read that your bank—or your
broker—is missing three million in securities from his vault
and can't account for the loss? Pretty sloppy way of running a
business, right? You lose a little faith. You begin to wonder.
You say, what the hell, why should I do business with an outfit
like that. And anyway the bank knows the loss is covered by
insurance."

He put the pipe down, interest kindling in his bespectacled
eyes, and started to look through one of the stacks on his desk.

"I'll give you an example of just that sort of thing; happened
to run across it the other day. . . . It's here somewhere."

Fenner watched with some amusement, pleased with himself as Sampson warmed to the subject. And considering the

amount of material cluttering his desk, the editor found what he wanted in a surprisingly short time. He gave a satisfied grunt of triumph and said:

"Here we are. Listen to this. From a feature in the New York *Daily News*. I'll quote exactly because this particular brokerage firm is no longer in business. You ready?

" 'A prime illustration,' " he read without waiting for a reply, " 'is the robbery at gunpoint of a Goodbody and Company messenger. Two men grabbed 34,800 shares in 100-share certificates of firms that included Ford, Cities Service, Northwest, and National Airlines from the eighteen-year-old delivery boy in broad daylight at Exchange Place and New Street.

" 'Two days later, Goodbody received a $2,034,631 check from Federal Insurance Company—the sum equal to the average market value of the stocks the day before the robbery. In return the broker transferred ownership of the stolen securities to the insurer. A spokesman for Federal spelled out the procedure.

" ' "Over the next ninety days or so, the transfer agents for the nine corporations that issued the stolen shares will replace them. The certificates will then be our property. As far as I can see our loss will be, in effect, the interest on the two million dollars for that period of time." ' "

Sampson tossed the clipping aside. "There you've got a good example. Farther along it says that hardly a week goes by that the New York Stock Exchange doesn't send out 'lost securities' flyers listing the missing paper."

The change in the editor's attitude was apparent. He seemed almost affable as he used three matches to light his pipe. Fenner waited until it was drawing properly before he spoke.

"That example took place a couple of years ago."

"Right but—"

"Did you happen to read about a similar case that occurred

in New York about two weeks back? The amount that time was three point eight million."

"I read it." Sampson removed his pipe, tipped his head, one eye half closing. "You think maybe that list of yours could be part of that loot?"

"My hunch—and that's all it is—says yes. The guy had a New York address. If he brought those certificates up from New York, and if he did they haven't been found, there has to be a reason for it."

Fenner sat up straighter so he could look over a foot-high stack of files and see Sampson better.

"Which brings up another point I'd like to get clear on. Some of the accounts I read mentioned hot and cold, or clean, stocks. What exactly is the difference?"

"Maybe forty percent," Sampson said, and grinned. "I mean that's one way of putting it. Hot stocks are the ones reported. The certificate numbers are listed in the flyers that go to brokerage houses and banks, some of them abroad. A lot of not so bright mob guys are doing time in Atlanta and Sing Sing and Dannemora for trying to peddle them. Cold stocks are the ones that go unreported, sometimes for a long time. They might be sold for up to fifty percent of the current value to someone who knows how to use them or has a market.

"Take that list you've got," he added. "Say the Mafia has someone in a bank or brokerage house who has access to the vault. With the right pressure this someone could be forced to match that list—which has to be hot because that theft was reported—with vault stocks that are from trust funds in the broker's custody and probably in the broker's name or a street name. Nobody but the guy who made the switch even knows the legitimate certificates are missing. Until they are sold. And only then because, if they are sold legitimately, the transfer agent, usually a big city bank, destroys that particular certificate and issues another to the new purchaser. So not until the original owner, who thinks his shares are at his bank or broker, misses a quarterly dividend and squawks would the broker think of checking the certificate number.

"And when he finds out the number is not the one he is supposed to have he knows a switch was made.

"And by that time," Sampson went on, "the guy who peddled the cold stock is long gone. But if that stock is used for collateral the transfer agent has no record of a sale, so the dividends keep right on coming to the legitimate owner. The broker, getting no complaints, still thinks he has the proper certificates in his vault. Until that stock is actually sold and the certificate turned into the transfer agent there's no way the switch can be discovered."

Fenner nodded, pleased with the corroboration of his tentative premise. To augment it still further he said:

"According to Alan Townsend every stock on that list is well known and traded daily."

"In thousands and tens of thousands of shares except for the higher priced ones."

"Millions of shares outstanding."

"Correct . . . Oh—" Sampson stopped as a new brightness touched his eyes and the beginning of his first smile lifted the corners of his mouth. "I see what you're driving at. You want to know if the local banks and some of the brokerage houses would have sufficient stocks in their custody to match the specific denominations of the certificates on your list, right?"

"Right."

"Any bank in town could duplicate that list many times over. And a few brokers too—I don't mean branches of New York firms." He named three of the most prominent local houses and Carter & Townsend was one of them.

Fenner nodded and stood up. He said if Sampson would explain one more thing he'd get out of his hair.

"I'm not sure just what a 'street name' is and what it means. What stocks I have I keep with Carter and Townsend so I won't have to run down to my safe deposit box and get the certificates every time I want to sell something. I assumed the shares were in the firm's name for easy transfer."

"They probably are." Sampson glanced at his dead pipe as though wondering whether it would be worthwhile to light it again. "Banks are more likely to use street names, the large ones. You want a for-instance?"

"Please."

"How much money would you say a bank like First Manhattan manages in personal trusts and especially pension funds?"

"Hundreds of millions?" Fenner's guess was tentative.

"Billions. So let's make up a company name, the XYZ Corporation. Millions of shares outstanding, worldwide holdings, maybe in natural resources. Also a market favorite. Now this may be an exaggeration—though I've seen figures on actual companies that come close—but because of those billions in trusts and pension funds the bank could be managing twenty percent of the total shares. Not owning it or controlling it but influencing decisions. Now you own twenty percent of an outfit like, say, U.S. Steel or Texaco and you have a lot of clout because no single stockholder, or any of the officers for that matter, owns as much as one percent."

He pointed the pipe again. "You can get your people on the board of directors, hire and fire management, raise or lower dividends. So some Congressman, or a bleeding-heart reporter, or any anti-business politician or troublemaker screams—on the air or in print—that this one bank owns twenty percent of one of the world's largest corporations. . . . Think of it, you clods! Jesus Christ, one lousy bank practically owns Republic Steel! . . . What a scandal, how unfair!" Sampson added with heavy sarcasm and, as though the very thought of such nonsense had left a bad taste in his mouth, finally gave up on the pipe.

"So to avoid that kind of unnecessary publicity, which is hardly a half-truth to begin with, the bank sets up a street name, maybe two. C. D. Jones . . . R. H. Smith and Co. All perfectly legal, registered with the proper county or state offices. But C. D. Jones becomes the nominal holder of seven percent of XYZ and Smith and Co. has another seven in its name. So now, though nothing has changed, First Manhattan appears on the company books as controlling only six percent. Less furor that way; nobody gives a damn. You get the idea?"

Fenner said he thought so. He thanked Sampson for his time and his information and said:

"I told Murdock to tell you I'd buy drinks, dinner, or both if you would see me, Mr. Sampson."

"Yeah. He told me."

"So how about it?"

Sampson still looked the academician but there was a new affability in his manner, his smile genuinely friendly now that he'd had a chance to share something of his knowledge with a sympathetic listener.

"Thanks," he said. "There have been times when I would have accepted such an offer gladly. But my stomach isn't what it used to be and my doctor says one good belt before dinner is my limit. My wife likes me to have that belt with her."

He stood up, stretched, and this time he shook hands.

9

It was 9:28 when Jack Fenner climbed the stone steps to the remodeled but ancient brownstone where he had his apartment. It was one of the few left in the quiet block, the other original buildings replaced or drastically face-lifted to serve as small business establishments. His current neighbors were a boutique, an antique shop, an artists' supply store, a professional photographer's studio, a tea room, and a second-floor dance studio.

He had dined in an obscure restaurant, partly to be alone so he could try to consolidate his information and his thoughts, partly because it was too late when he thought of it to phone either of two women friends, who, when given sufficient warning, their moods at the time compatible, seemed happy to have his company. One was a widow with two small children, the other a divorcee, both in their early thirties; neither eager to remarry but usually willing to share an evening or an occasional night with him. Theirs was a warm, friendly, sometimes intimate relationship that continued to be unemotional but mutually satisfying. But one didn't just drop in on them; you telephoned in advance like any proper gentleman.

Because the early fall night was clear and pleasantly crisp, he had walked the five blocks from the garage, reminding himself to have Alice Maxwell mail in his traffic citation and the fine, thereby avoiding an appearance in court. He noticed nothing unusual when he opened the downstairs door, which seldom latched properly—no great danger since outwardly the old building seemed an unlikely prospect for any intelligent burglar.

The lower-floor apartment, rented by two middle-aged schoolteachers, was quiet as usual as he climbed to his second-floor quarters. The elderly couple that lived above him was seldom seen or heard. He unlocked his door automatically, his mind wandering.

Unfortunately, though under the circumstances it probably made no difference, he had no intuitive warning nor did he sense that anything was wrong or out of the ordinary until he stepped through the little entryway and flicked the light switch. Only then did he pull up stiffly and gape at the man sitting in one of the club chairs, hat and coat still on, a relaxed, heavy-set fellow with a smirk on his rubbery face and a heavy-looking gun in his lap.

"Come in, come in." The voice was insolent, and as the smirk became a grin the man lifted the gun and waved it carelessly. "We flicked off the lights when we heard the downstairs door. We figured to finish before you showed. Pretty early for a bachelor like you, ain't it?"

Fenner, at first a victim of surprise and outraged indignation at this open violation of his privacy, felt the first stirrings of resentment. The moment over, he took time to inspect the rest of the room, considering with some pride the comfortable divan, the two club chairs, the winged chair, the etchings and lithographs on the walls. The orientals were secondhand but good, the maple dropleaf table and the two end tables were genuine antiques, the rest of the pieces satisfactory reproductions. Only one thing appeared to have been disturbed. The drawers of the kneehole desk were not as he had left them and he noted this before his cold narrowed gaze came back to his visitor.

"What the hell do you want?" he demanded, certain now that he had seen this man before and trying to place him.

"Just having a quick look for something." The man, not turning his head then yelled, "Hey, you guys!"

They appeared at once in the opening to the short hall that led to the bedroom and kitchen. Both were young, of medium height, one somewhat stockier than the other. Fenner had been familiar with the type for years: odd-job hoodlums recruited from the streets and anxious to prove their worth to those more important in the chain of mob command. He had never seen either of them but he would know them again with their blue jackets and slacks that flared at the cuffs like sailor pants, confident, cocky, contemptuous, one with sleek black hair and sideburns, the stocky one with tangled, tightly curled dark hair grown long, uncombed and snarled, apparently modeled on so many of the crop of juveniles currently in favor with television producers and casting directors.

"You find it yet?" The seated man was still eyeing Fenner.

"Nothing in the kitchen," the stocky one said. "Unless you want to count juice, instant coffee, booze, or powdered milk."

"But I did find this," his companion said.

Something in the tone made the boss take a quick look. So did Fenner, recognizing the Smith & Wesson .38 that was now dangling from the youth's fingers.

"Where'd you find it?" The big man sounded annoyed.

"Table drawer, next to the bed."

"Well, put it back, goddamn it! Right where you found it! And wipe it off, understand? You know what we want, and we leave things neat. . . . Go ahead, Fenner," he added. "Sit down somewhere. Get comfortable. It shouldn't be too long now."

He waved the gun again to indicate the room. "We already tossed this room. Closet too." He pointed at the vestibule closet. "Hardly know it, would you? Keep it neat, that's my motto."

Fenner, who had stood unmoving the past couple of minutes, considered the suggestion. He was seething inside as he weighed odds, but except for his flinty stare and the tightened muscles at the hinge of his jaws it did not show. In the end he knew that any chance for action on his part was exceedingly remote.

It was not just the threat of the gun or the fact that the man handled it with an easy familiarity; it was the thought that even if he somehow managed to get close enough to neutralize it he would have to contend with the other two, who most likely were carrying weapons of their own; that type usually did. And so he began to move, easily, purposely giving the man plenty of room as he headed for the divan.

The other turned with him, the gun swiveling as he did so and suddenly the mental association Fenner had been seeking came to him and he felt like the ancient Greek who had shouted, "Eureka!" For he had the man's name now; he also recalled the occasions when he had noticed him.

Fiori.

The first name escaped him, if he ever knew it. A hanger-on not unlike his two younger associates but with more muscle and some seniority. Fenner had no idea whether or not he had a record but that would be easy to check with Lieutenant Bacon. More important was the company he kept.

It was for this reason that Fenner had noticed him in the first place. At the track, or the lobby of the Garden when the Celtics or the Bruins were playing. Talking to others not unlike him, occasionally in the company of a man named Maurie Matlock, whose chief occupation, now that he had risen from a small-time Shylock to a man of substance, was the loaning of funds in a way that had made him part owner of various small businesses, a couple of apartments, a provider of capital for a large condominium project out West Roxbury way. Now, deciding it would do no harm to pry some, Fenner said:

"What the hell does Maurie want? What did he tell you to look for?"

Fiori let his thick brows climb and his look of innocence was comical.

"Maurie? Maurie who?"

"Matlock, you stupid bastard!"

Fiori shrugged, taking no offense. "Never heard of him, Fenner."

"Still on the payroll, or just freelance jobs like this?"

Fiori grunted contemptuously. "What're you smoking these days? Pot? Hash? . . . Hey in there," he yelled. "How much longer?"

A voice from the bedroom called back, "Just finishing."

Fiori stood up, adjusted his narrow-brimmed felt. He let the gun hang at his side but his little eyes remained alert as he waited for his companions. They appeared a minute later, the stocky one opening both hands in front of him, palms up.

"Zilch."

Fenner, helpless, frustrated, and impotent, stood up as the three moved toward the entryway. Aware that threats would be futile he finally said:

"Tell Matlock I'll be around to see him."

"You tell him," Fiori replied with some malice. "You're the guy what knows him."

"You know I'll report this," Fenner said, still quietly fuming.

"Sure. And me and Al and Gino will have alibis the F.B.I. couldn't break in four years. . . . So long, Fenner."

Fiori was at the entryway now but Al or Gino—Fenner did not know which was which, but it was the thin one with the slick hair—couldn't let well enough alone. Moving in front of Fenner he sneered at him.

"They told us," he said, "that you might be trouble. You know, a real heavy cat." He chuckled. "More like a pussy-cat—"

Fenner finished the sentence for him. It was a short right hook with weight behind it. Al or Gino, who had no warning, sat down, blinking hard, not hurt but momentarily stunned. As he started to rise Fiori snarled at him.

"You wouldn't listen, would you, you stupid shit!" he said furiously. "Get up! Come on, goddamn it, let's go while you've still got your health."

Fenner sat down again after he heard the door close. His anger in hand now, he gently massaged the knuckles of his hand, finding some satisfaction in the blow even though in a certain sense it was a childish demonstration. Then, his mind moving on, he considered a theory that was at least acceptable in its premise. It centered on the probability that the murdered Leslie Ludlow had come to town with four hundred thousand in hot stocks.

Such a conclusion led to other acceptable probabilities. If indeed Fiori was doing this job for Matlock, it seemed likely that he had been searching for the bulky envelope last seen when Ludlow's girlfriend slipped it from under the mattress at the Starlight Motel.

It would follow then that Matlock knew of Ludlow's trip to the city and its purpose, which would further suggest that Matlock had the sort of New York connections that would designate him as the local representative to handle or oversee a stock swap if one was to be made.

All this, Fenner realized, was predicated on his hunch that Ludlow was carrying stock as a messenger or courier, and that it was part of the three-million-plus theft that had been set up two or three weeks earlier in New York.

He pushed himself erect finally, aware that much of this was supposition. But the parts fitted. And what the hell else did he have?

As he moved to the kitchen to build a nightcap he decided that Bacon would have to be told tomorrow. But in return, if he played his hand right and didn't get the lieutenant mad, he could expect a reasonably accurate assessment of what Ludlow had been doing for a living and who his associates were in New York. If he had a record there, which seemed likely, that information might be of some help.

He took his Scotch-and-water into the bedroom, peering suspiciously around to see if Al and Gino had made a mess of things. It helped some to see that only the bedclothes showed signs of their presence. The spread was mussed and the pillows out of place. He understood this since a bed or some part of it was a likely hiding place for an envelope such as he had in mind.

Satisfied that there were no other signs of disorder, he went first to the bedside table and took his .38 from the drawer; he even dumped the shells into his palm before reinserting them. Reassured, he began to undress, hanging up his coat and trousers properly and with his customary neatness. When he came back naked from the bathroom, he straightened the sheets and slid between them.

He took a small sip of his drink and placed the glass where he could reach it in the dark before he turned off the lamp. For perhaps three minutes while his resentment and indignation faded and he considered plans for the following day, a sort of haze enveloped his mind. Two minutes later he was sound asleep, the rest of his drink forgotten and untouched.

10

THE SHARP RING of the telephone brought Jack Fenner out of
that half-world of the brain that exists just before sleep touches
the borders of wakefulness. Because he had rested well and
had no recollection of any dreams, he rolled over and grabbed
for the handset in the middle of the second ring, already wide
awake, his sense of physical fitness such that he was not even
annoyed by the shrill interruption.

"Yeah," he said, glancing at the small electric clock to see
that it was already ten minutes after nine.

"Mr. Fenner." The voice was Alice Maxwell's, and unlike
her normal cheerful manner he thought he detected a cadence
that seemed both apologetic and uncertain. "I didn't wake
you, did I?"

"No," Fenner lied. "I just started to dress. Is something
wrong?"

"Well, yes. I just came in. I thought I'd call right away."

He could hear her take a small breath, waited, finally
prompted her. "Yes, Alice."

"Someone was here last night."

Fenner considered the announcement and found it ambiguous. When there was no further elaboration, he said with
studied patience:

"You mean someone broke in?"

"Well, not exactly," she said, sounding like a conscientious child not sure how to explain a difficult situation. "I mean, the doors weren't forced. Someone must have a key or something. I didn't suspect anything until I unlocked your private office and saw your filing cabinet."

"Oh?"

"The top drawer, where the lock is? Well, someone had pried it out of shape and broke it. The lock, I mean. And of course that unlocked the other drawers and—"

"And the files were all scattered around," Fenner finished, visualizing the worst.

"Oh, no. Everything seemed to be there. Only not so neat of course. And then I noticed the desk."

Fenner took a labored breath, afraid to speculate until he blew it out.

"What about the desk, Alice?"

"The center drawer was forced. The wood is sort of scratched, you know, around the lock. I couldn't tell if anything was missing."

"Okay, don't worry about it. Call the insurance man; you have his number somewhere. Ask him to stop by and take a look. Don't bother with the police. I'll be seeing Lieutenant Bacon later. . . . One more thing," he added, his brain already in high gear and functioning smoothly. "Call Tom Valano. If he's not in, leave word with his answering service to call me."

"Here?"

"Yes. I'll be there in a half hour."

He hung up and scratched his scalp absently as he sat on the edge of the bed, already having an idea of what was behind the break-in. He wasted another second or two wondering if the filing cabinet would have to be replaced. It had never been guaranteed against burglars, only against fire. Well, the hell with it . . .

Alice Maxwell was at her desk sorting the mail when Fenner entered and the first thing he noticed was the throw rug she had purchased the day before to cover the bloodstains. It was a complementary shade of green and went well with the wall-to-wall carpet it covered.

* Alice had stopped her sorting and was watching him now and he was reminded again how very attractive she was with her soft blond hair, the smooth pink-and-white complexion, the wide-spaced blue eyes. Her usual bubbly manner had temporarily deserted her as she awaited his reaction, and she had a subdued, almost guilty look, as though what had happened was her fault.

To cheer her up he gave a big smile and an affectionate squeeze on her shoulder. He told her not to worry about a thing, and asked if she had been able to reach the insurance man.

"He said he'd stop in some time today."

"Good enough. And Valano?"

"I left word with his answering service. He's expected in any time."

In his office with Alice lingering in the doorway, Fenner saw at once that the job done on the locking mechanism of the filing cabinet had been amateurish but effective, the metal around the lock bent out of shape, probably by a pry bar. The desk bothered him more because the scars around the lock were deep and ugly and it would call for an expert refinisher to make it look right.

He opened and closed the drawers, not looking for anything, noting a certain messiness but nothing he hadn't expected. If anything was missing it was not at once apparent, and now in his chair he picked up the telephone and nodded his dismissal.

When Alice retreated he opened the top right-hand drawer and found a private address book, flipped to the indexed page, and began to dial.

He had done a lot of thinking on his way to the office. It was again a pleasant morning and, having no plans for his car that day, he found the walk served to stimulate his thinking. He had his juice, coffee, and Danish at a drugstore counter and by

the time he turned into his building he had formulated a vague
theory that seemed worth exploring. The premise was based
mostly on hearsay and rumor that he had picked up here and
there over the past couple of years. What he hoped for now
was some verification. . . .

"Bryant's Dry Cleaning." The voice at the other end was
husky and impatient.

"Teddy? Jack Fenner."

"Hey, Jack." The tone became more friendly. "You been
taking your action some place else?"

"Would I do a thing like that? I've been waiting for a sure
thing."

"With only sure things I'd be out of business."

Fenner chuckled to show he appreciated the remark and
visualized the little man at the other end of the wire. Bryant's
Dry Cleaning was Teddy Breen, a longtime bookie who had
been content to operate with an established clientele, never
infringing on the turf of others, paying his dues, keeping his
nose clean. He had only been busted once since Fenner had
known him. He paid his fine, waited an appropriate interval,
and opened shop at a new location.

"I phoned early," Fenner said, "before the action starts so
we could talk a minute. Take those other two phones off the
hook, will you? I need some help."

"What kind of help?" Teddy said, at once suspicious.

"You get around. You pretty much know what's going on."

"So?"

"Do you know a guy named Bruce Townsend?"

"The broker fellow? I've seen him. I don't do business with
him. He ain't a horse player anyway."

"I've seen him at the track a couple of times."

"A five-and-ten-dollar bettor, strictly at the windows."

"I heard somewhere that he was in kind of heavy to
someone."

"I heard that too."

"From what? Floating games? Charter flights?"

"I hear he took one a few years back. No, the way I get it the guy's a football nut."

"If he's in as heavy as I hear," Fenner said, embellishing the rumor, "he must have some markers out. Is he getting the vigorish up?"

"I ain't read anywhere that he had any arms broke so he must be taking care of it."

"You wouldn't know who holds those markers?"

"I could guess but I'm not about to. . . . Look, Jack. You're holding me up. You could be costing me action."

"Not at this hour, not that much action. So keep those other two phones off the hook and listen."

"Jesus, Jack! They're my bread and butter."

"I know. I also know you've got friends who hear things. I've got some friends too."

"So?"

"So one of my friends could close you down at say 3:05 this afternoon. Just when business is booming."

"All right, all right. They're off the hook, goddamn it!"

"Good. Now if you had to guess, if someone was twisting your arm, who would you say might be holding those heavy markers of Bruce Townsend's?"

"As a guess?"

"As a guess."

"Could be Maurie Matlock, is what I'd guess."

"What was it that put him in that big?"

"Somebody said he took the big fall on the Super Bowl game."

"The last one?"

"Year before. Miami-Minnesota."

"And he's not clean yet?"

"I hear no."

"Thanks, Teddy. Put the phones back on. Next time I see you remind me I owe you a couple drams, okay?"

He hung up and leaned back, his frown biting deeply at his

forehead and giving his green eyes a squinty look. Before he could begin to collate this information Alice buzzed him and said Mr. Valano was on the line.

Tom Valano, a tall, skinny, bearded youth, was a wizard with a camera. As a teenager he had been freelancing for the local papers and wire services and when he was old enough he had managed to get a private investigator's license not because he ever intended to investigate anything but because it opened up a new field of prospective clients, Fenner being one of his first.

"Jack?" he said now. "My answering service said I was to phone you."

"Right, Tom. Could you do a small job for me today?"

"Well—" There was regret in the tone as Valano hesitated. "I kind of doubt it, Jack. I'm on a couple of things now that I ought to—"

"You eat lunch, don't you?"

"Well, sure. Mostly."

"So this will take half your lunch hour if I can set it up. Where will you be in fifteen minutes?"

"Right here. My office."

"Stay there. I'll call you back."

As soon as the connection broke Fenner dialed a more familiar number. When the female voice said, "Good morning, Carter and Townsend," he said, "Mr. Abbott, please."

When Abbott came on Fenner identified himself and said:

"George? Do me a favor, will you? A bit of information and never mind why I want it, okay? What time does Bruce usually go out to lunch?"

"Usually twelve-thirty, give or take a couple of minutes, unless he has a client lunch."

"Could you ask his secretary if he's got a date for today? No reason why you have to tell her why you want to know, is there?"

"Not that I know of. It's a normal sort of question. Hang

on." It took no more than fifteen seconds for Abbott to come back with an answer. "She says no lunch date so far today. Of course he could make one later in the morning."

"That's okay, George. Thanks. When I build up my bank account I'll be calling you. Maybe you can find me a sleeper."

Once again he broke the connection and dialed. When Tom Valano answered Fenner said, "It's all set. A half-hour is all I need. Grab a pencil and write down this address. . . . Got it? Okay, meet me across the street from there at twelve-fifteen. And bring that camera that can adjust up to three hundred millimeters or whatever—"

Valano's laugh cut him off. "Look, Jack," he said patiently, "let me be the photographer, okay? Just tell me what you want."

The relevance of the remark brought an answering chuckle from Fenner. Telling Valano what camera to use or how to take a picture was like telling Henry Aaron how to swing a bat or Sonny Jurgensen how to throw a pass.

Fenner told him what he had in mind and Valano asked one question. "Prevailing street light? The guy's not supposed to know he's being shot?"

"Right. Twelve-fifteen."

Fenner thought a moment after he hung up. Then, pursuing the same tenuous line of thought, he again referred to his address file and dialed still another number, this time to a friend of his in the motor vehicle department, a veteran by the name of Frawley.

"Sam?" he said when he had his man. "Jack Fenner."

"Well, what do you know. It's been a long time, Jack. What have you got for me, a couple of freebies to a Patriots game?"

Fenner laughed and said he might have before the season was over. "Got a pencil? Bruce Townsend, this city. What kind of a car do you have him registered as owning?"

"Hold on," Frawley said, "while I punch some buttons."

Fenner leaned back while he waited and began to make a one-handed examination of the mail Alice had put on his desk, tossing the junk pieces into the wastebasket and separating the bills from the two or three envelopes that needed attention.

"Yeah," he said a minute later.

"A 1972 Mercedes 350 SL. Two-door, gray."

"Thanks, Sam. I owe you."

Frawley chuckled, said he would remember, and rang off.

11

WHEN JACK FENNER walked into the squad room outside
Lieutenant Bacon's office he was reminded again how un-
changed the place was. His trips here were infrequent these
days but it seemed that there were always two detectives
present yet never more than three. He did not know exactly
how many men made up this particular squad but of the
present pair one was reading a newspaper and the other
pecking away on a typewriter as he worked on some report.
This one did not even glance up as Fenner passed; the one
with the paper lowered it long enough for a peek but made no
comment as Fenner headed for the open door.

Once inside he closed the door immediately and leaned
back against it, waiting for the lieutenant to look up from the
open file on his desk and acknowledge his presence. When
Bacon did lift his head his frown was openly disapproving but
not unexpected.

"I'm kind of busy," he growled, leaning back.

Fenner nodded, unperturbed, and glanced around the small
office with its old oak desk, matching chair with cushion, two
visitors' chairs, also of oak. A map filled part of one wall, as did
a blackboard another. The single window had no view.

"I know," Fenner said dryly. "You have my sympathy. I just
thought you'd take a minute to tell me what kind of a package

you have on Leslie Ludlow. After all, I identified him for you."

"With a full set of prints and his record we'd have pegged him anyway."

"Did you send a man out to talk to the motel owner?"

"Sure. Your story checked out."

"So why not let me in on Ludlow's background? What the hell's the matter with you? You want cooperation, give a little."

Bacon tipped his chin a half inch to one side and speculative glints appeared in the gray eyes. "You got anything left to trade?"

Fenner sighed heavily to make sure the sound was heard. He shook his head and spoke in plaintive, injured tones.

"I don't know why you can't be like the homicide lieutenants on television."

Bacon seemed to sense that he was being set up but his curiosity proved stronger than any tendency he may have had to ignore the remark.

"What's that crack supposed to mean?"

"Well, take a look sometime. You take Mannix, Cannon, even old Barnaby Jones. With them the homicide lieutenant is a pal. They're buddy-buddy. Tell the private eye everything he wants to know, open up the files, help him solve his case, even against regulations. Not only that but every lab man and specialist leans over backward to cooperate. But you—"

Fenner was unable to embellish the imagery because for once Bacon laughed, a hearty but genuine bellow that was seldom heard in those parts. When he got his breath he proved that he too had a sense of humor.

"You want to know why, I'll tell you. I'm no actor, right? I don't have a writer or a script and this isn't television. So just answer my question."

"You mean about having something to trade? Yeah, I think so."

"And you're not going to pass it along unless I play ball."

"Maybe eventually but not now."

Bacon nodded, a tiny smile tugging at the corners of his mouth, as though he had expected some such reply but wanted confirmation. It was simply a game that had to be played before he could in good conscience release private information to an outsider.

"New York had a package on him," he said, bending over the file again. "Nothing big. The F.B.I. more or less duplicates it and the Cincinnati people have a small sheet of their own."

"So he came originally from Ohio?"

"Born there. One arrest for extortion. Ninety days, suspended. Worked as a credit bureau investigator. To keep their jobs those guys have to turn in a certain number of reports daily. Eventually he was caught zinging some, so—"

"Zinging?" Fenner pushed away from the door and sat down. "That's one I don't know."

"You oughta," Bacon said smugly. "A young fellow like you with a thriving business. You've made a lot of checks yourself."

"Thanks for the young."

"The term is relative."

"Admitted."

"Like I say some credit bureaus do business on a quota basis. Not the better known ones, but some. You want to keep your job or get ahead, you turn in ten or a dozen or whatever reports a day. How many do you think you could do right in an eight-hour day?"

Bacon expected no answer nor did he wait for one. "Zinging means when you fake some, make up some of the answers to save time; instead of asking all a guy's neighbors about his character and standing, ask maybe one.

"But there's another side to that racket too. A prejudiced opinion, a bad rating can hurt a guy's standing for years; get him turned down for credit, maybe cost him his job. So maybe the investigator goes to the guy and says he'll withhold some damaging bit of information for a hundred or two or whatever.

That's how Ludlow got hit with the extortion charge."

"A real clean-cut, ethical character."

Bacon nodded and turned another sheet in the folder. "Married some dame that worked for the same company. Started playing the field and she caught him at it and put a slug in him. Lucky for both of them the wound wasn't serious. Between the lung and shoulder blade, a nice clean hole."

He stopped again and Fenner, knowing there was more, remained silent and very still.

"He was only in the hospital a week. They held the wife on an open charge until they knew Ludlow'd be okay. Released her on a two thousand bond. She got a bail bondsman to put it up and then jumped. Nobody gave a damn except the bondsman; he's probably still looking for her."

"How long ago?"

"Three years."

"So what did you get on Mrs. Ludlow?"

"There is no Mrs. Ludlow except the one I just mentioned. The description you gave me of the chick Ludlow brought up here with him fits the one he's been living with in New York. Some young go-go dancer. Her name is Hildy Dryden. No record on file. Nothing on where she came from yet except some neighbor said he thought it was Ohio. That checks with what her former boss said."

"When did Ludlow move in on New York?"

Bacon turned another page in the file. "After he got probation on the extortion in Cincinnati and the company fired him. He could have had some sort of connection in New York because the first the local law knows about him he's picked up in a gambling raid. Apparently worked as a small-time bookie for an Upper West Side mob. Got away with fines the first two times. Did thirty days on Rikers Island finally, the only time he fell. Nothing heavy on his sheet. No muscle. The word is that recently he's been acting as some sort of courier for the syndicate—"

"Wouldn't that explain why he was in town?"

"If we knew what he was carrying, and why. It wouldn't explain why he got it in your office." Bacon spread his hands, adding a bit of needle. "Unless of course it was you he expected to contact."

Fenner let the crack go by, his features expressionless as he brought forth the carbon of the list he had found in Ludlow's extra suit. He knew there might be a small explosion when he explained the circumstances but he knew Bacon's displeasure would be only temporary if he talked convincingly enough. Now he watched the lieutenant unfold the sheet, examine it, scowl at it, and then transfer the scowl to Fenner.

"What the hell is this?"

Fenner told him. When Bacon asked where all the figures came from Fenner told him that too. Then came the two questions he had been waiting for.

"Where did you get this—and when?"

"Ludlow had a suit hanging in the motel closet. I'd been giving the room a toss and when I searched the suit I found this carbon in the inside pocket of his jacket. I had it unfolded and was taking a quick glance, not knowing just what it meant, when the girl walked in on me like I told you before.

"I didn't have time to do anything but jam it in my side pocket and hope she didn't see me," he added, illustrating by repeating the movement. "Practically a reflex action. After that I was too busy handling her. I'm thinking all the way to my place and while I shave and shower. I put on the same jacket and when I get to my office I find the sweet old guy across the hall is already on his way to the morgue.

"You tell me to go back to my office and I do, sick inside and hating the guy that did it. I've got no time to remember the sheet or anything else. Young Lipscomb is there and we talk and he asks me to work on the case. Not until you've asked all your questions and I'm alone do I stick my hand in my pocket and find the sheet."

"You could have called me then," Bacon said accusingly.

"I could have but I didn't," Fenner said, standing his

ground. "I wanted to know what those symbols and figures added up to."

"And you were too goddamn busy after that to come in with what you learned. That's the only reason, hunh?"

"If you want the truth, no." Fenner looked right at Bacon and his grin came in spite of himself. "Because I know you. I knew damn well when I came in this morning you'd hem and haw and stall around. With you cooperation is a one-way street. Before you give out with anything a guy needs something to trade, right? Come on, admit it."

Bacon's grumble was a growling sound without words. He dropped his gaze, opened a drawer, and removed one of his vile-smelling panatelas, fingered it a moment; then he put it aside unlit. When he was ready he looked up, not quite shamefaced but no longer belligerent.

"So I got a job to do," he said. "I do it my way when I can."

Fenner lit a cigarette, dropped the match carefully in the desk ashtray, and remained mute. Bacon turned to stare at the brick wall beyond his window. This went on for perhaps two minutes. But he was too good a detective to let a minor irritation or setback influence his better judgment and now he was ready to pursue an intelligent line of questioning.

"So your hunch says that maybe Ludlow came to town with around four hundred grand in stocks. If he was just a courier someone in New York supplied that stock. You got any ideas on that?"

"A couple," Fenner said, and told of his research and the confirmations that had come from his session with Fred Sampson at the *Courier*. When he also mentioned the recent hold-up of a broker's messenger in New York City he added, "My guess is that Ludlow's package was part of the three point eight million heist."

Bacon's brow was furrowed now as he grappled mentally with what apparently were new facts and suppositions. He groped for and found his cigar, and this time he lit it. Fenner waited until he could be sure of the lieutenant's attention.

"You said yourself the hit looked like a professional job. So maybe someone up here, not the one Ludlow was supposed to make delivery to, found out about the meeting and came to make the hit and grab the loot—"

"Or," Bacon added, "maybe someone not exactly trusting Ludlow wanted to make sure he'd never talk."

Fenner accepted the statement without comment, all too aware of the enormous hole in both suppositions. That hole was based on his own knowledge that Ludlow's girlfriend, now known as Hildy Dryden, had a bulky envelope that very likely contained the missing certificates. Which left two quite different but still reasonable assumptions—she had shot Ludlow and run with the stock, or whoever did kill him had either overlooked or ignored that envelope.

Such knowledge now presented a problem. He did not see it as one of ethics as much as one of obligation. This point reminded him of the difference between him and Bacon, a subject he had considered frequently ever since he left the force. There were, he knew, both advantages and disadvantages to his present status.

Bacon's sworn duty was to enforce the law, to follow proper procedures, to question all suspects in whatever manner seemed best, to make arrests when evidence warranted such a step. For that he had security and a reasonable pension to look forward to.

Fenner had no such security. In his old age he could count on only what he had been able to put aside, plus social security. On the other hand he enjoyed a certain freedom of action denied a law officer. He was not sworn to enforce the law but only to obey it. Loyalty to a client was a primary concern and he could not be made to divulge information given confidentially, except in court. It was not his job to make arrests and he had no more authority to do so than the average citizen. That he had on occasion held a likely suspect until the arrival of the police was beside the point.

In this instance, insofar as he knew, only he and Hildy

Dryden were aware of the existence of that envelope. Since a client's interests were not presently involved, he had no good reason to withhold this information.

When he had stubbed out his cigarette, not looking at Bacon, not looking at anything, he said, hoping it would sound like an afterthought:

"There's one other thing I noticed in that motel room."

Bacon sat up, traces of suspicion again flickering in his gray gaze. "So let's have it."

Fenner spoke of the envelope then, detailing the circumstances. "I had to sit and watch her pack," he finished. "That envelope she had hidden under the mattress was the last thing she put in the suitcase."

"What kind of an envelope?"

Fenner described it, adding, "It looked bulky enough to hold quite a few stock certificates. If that's what Ludlow brought to town."

"What the hell. She could have done the job, couldn't she?"

"It's possible."

"And you just happened to think of it, right?" Bacon's sarcasm was pointed. "You had no idea that envelope could be important?"

"It wasn't important until I began to understand why Ludlow came here and what he could have brought with him." Fenner's tone was flat and challenging, so was the look in his eyes. "So don't get snotty. Maybe it's important, maybe not. If you pick up the girl—and that's your job, isn't it?—and if she still has that envelope, then you'll know how important it is."

He stood up, bristling some now. "What the hell are you crabbing about? I didn't have to tell you anything and you know it. I've already given you more than—"

"All right, all right." Bacon held up one hand, his tone placating. "It's another lead maybe." He thought a moment, his attitude doing a turnabout. "Lead? Hell, she could be it! She comes up from New York, already knowing what Ludlow's carrying. Follows him to your office Saturday morning."

He paused again. He said, "Yeah," mostly to himself and seemed almost gleeful at the new prospect. He even dry-washed his hands as he expounded.

"She does the job—and for all we know that could have been something she'd had on her mind for quite a while—turns out his pockets with some idea we won't identify him. Grabs the envelope and blows. Sure, why not?" he asked, and waited for some confirmation.

The impulse to grin was hard to control but Fenner mastered it. He nodded, his tone serious but not enthusiastic.

"A possibility. What bothers me a little is why didn't she take off? Why wait around all weekend?"

"That," said Bacon, "is something we'll find out when we pick her up. The precinct squads have their snitches working the streets. It shouldn't be too long. This way we can narrow it down a bit." He half closed one eye and said, "Or maybe you've got another theory or two we haven't discussed. You usually have."

Fenner thought it over, but not for long. What theories he had were still too tenuous to mention. He could not discuss them, nor could he reveal certain incipient suspicions until he could substantiate them. Right now he could not in good conscience pass along to Bacon, or anyone else, theories unsupported by facts. Personal hunches were best kept to himself lest someone, suspected but innocent, be badly hurt unnecessarily. This was an area on which he trod lightly. If and when the time came to reveal what he suspected he would accept the consequences.

"No theories." He paused, a half-smile on his face. "Would you settle for a couple of facts?"

"Like what?"

Fenner spoke of the three visitors of the night before. He detailed what they did and what was said. He described the two younger men and said he had never seen either of them.

"But I made the guy with the gun," he added. "Name's Fiori. I've seen him with Maurie Matlock."

Bacon nodded and allowed himself to look rather pleased at the new information.

"Sure," he said. "It can be made to fit. Fiori's been up a half-dozen times for assault and extortion. Fell once. Did eighteen months at Walpole. And Matlock?" His tone was musing, a faraway gleam in his eyes. "Stolen securities, hot or cold, could be used to finance some of that construction he's supposed to be financing."

"There's more." Fenner waited until the lieutenant's glance came back to him and focused. He then spoke of the break-in at his office, the broken locks on his filing cabinet and desk. "That wouldn't have to be Fiori," he said. "Matlock—if he is behind this—could have brought in someone else."

Bacon nodded, speculating. "We could pick up Fiori," he said without much conviction.

"No point. Matlock's mouthpiece would spring him in two hours. And anyway he'll have an alibi that will stand up. He won't talk. You know that. He's been through the mill before."

"Yeah," Bacon said, as though he had not heard. He leaned back, eyes half closed. "And the only reason I can come up with that makes any sense, that would explain why anyone would want to toss your place—and office—is because Matlock figures maybe you found the envelope when you discovered the body." He swiveled his chair to stare out the window. "And so far there ain't anything but your story to say he's wrong."

It was not an accusation. There was no challenge or conviction in the tone and Fenner took no offense. The words were those of a veteran law officer thinking aloud and schooled never to ignore a possibility no matter how unlikely.

Understanding this, Fenner got up and moved over to the door. Bacon did not seem to notice. He was somehow in a trance of his own making as he considered the new information and the possibilities it opened up. Fenner went out quietly, not even sure that Bacon saw him leave. . . .

·   ·   ·

Tom Valano, lanky and bearded, was standing beside his car when Fenner paid off the taxi at twenty-two minutes after twelve. A parking meter street with a twenty-minute limit meant that spaces opened frequently and Valano had been lucky to find one for his coupe almost directly across the street from the entrance to Carter & Townsend. Fenner shook hands and complimented him and Valano said he'd been lucky.

"If we feed the meter we can stay here until your man shows. So what's the situation?"

Fenner told him and Valano reached through the rolled-down window and took from the front seat a camera with an extended lens. With elbows on the car roof, he focused carefully. He pointed out the opening between two cars parked across the pavement.

"If I have enough warning I should be able to get a couple shots full length. When he starts walking the rest will be from the waist up only." Fenner said that would be good enough and they waited, eyes on the shadowed entryway.

They got a small break when Bruce Townsend appeared a few minutes later because he paused as he stepped out on the sidewalk, as people often do, with a glance up and down the street as though it took a while to orient himself before deciding which way to turn.

Having already been given a description of Townsend, Valano spotted him the same moment Fenner did. Fenner said, "The tall blond," and Valano said, "Got him," and Fenner could hear the shutter click, saw the quick movement as the film was advanced to the next frame.

Townsend had appeared in the company of another representative like George Abbott, whom Fenner recognized but did not know, and by the time the pair was out of focus he knew Valano had taken at least a half-dozen exposures.

"Good work, Tom," he said when Valano lowered the camera.

"Three or four of them should be okay," Valano said modestly. "How much do you want them blown?"

"From the waist up should do, or head and shoulders. A couple of each maybe; well cropped."

"Eight-by-tens?"

"Shouldn't need them that big if you bring them up enough. Four-by-fives are easier to carry. So when can you deliver them?" He gave Valano a smile and a light squeeze on the arm. "A special job is worth a bonus."

"If I wet print I should have them for you in thirty or forty minutes. Your office?"

"I'll be there," Fenner said, stepping out to flag a cab. "And thanks, kid. Appreciate it."

12

By the time Jack Fenner returned to his office Alice Maxwell had gone out to lunch and once at his desk he dialed Klinger's Delicatessen and asked for Eddie, the delivery boy.

"Eddie," he said when he had identified himself. "What's good today?"

"Everything," Eddie said. "Like always."

"Anything fresh roasted this morning?"

"Chickens. Maybe even still warm."

"Great. On white bread. A double coffee."

"Light with no sugar, right? Coming right over . . ."

Tom Valano arrived as Fenner was finishing the last of his coffee. Alice had not yet returned but Fenner had made notes on the three letters that required a reply. One congratulated him on a small job and asked for a bill, and after he consulted his time records he penciled in a figure for Alice. The second letter was a query from a law firm suggesting a consultation and asking for an appointment. The third came from the largest private security firm in town offering him a job.

The half-smile on Valano's long thin face told Fenner all he really had to know and the young photographer slipped the prints out of the envelope with pride.

Fenner spread the nine prints and saw that there were three each of three different exposures, almost lifelike in their glossy clarity and Fenner marveled at such expertise.

"Beautiful," he said. "Did you bring a bill?"

Valano, producing it, said, "Fifty bucks. I added a little extra on account of—"

Fenner cut him off. "This kind of work is worth fifty bucks." As he started to reach for his personal checkbook Alice came in and walked over to his doorway. She knew Valano and said hello and gave him her bright friendly smile. Tom blushed a little and said hello and Fenner returned Valano's bill.

"Give it to Alice, will you? . . . A check for fifty for Mr. Valano—for services rendered . . . And Alice," he added before she could withdraw, "when you can, phone the travel agency downstairs and see if Marge is in. If so ask her how busy she is, and if she can see me if I come down."

He leaned back, an unconscious smile on his mouth as his mind dwelt in succession on the excellent sandwich, the highly successful assignment Valano had just completed, the forthcoming chat with Marge. When the outer door closed on Valano he became aware that his daydreaming had resulted in a nice feeling of self-satisfaction and he wondered if it was justified.

He listened with one ear to Alice's telephone conversation. Presently she replaced the instrument and stuck her head in the doorway, her small smile impish.

"Marge says to tell you to hurry. She's waiting with bated breath."

Fenner chuckled, thanked her, and gave her instructions on how to answer the three letters. He said he would probably be back after he had seen Marge and if not, he would call her. . . .

Marge Tyler was at the front of the counter near the window, her fully packed but shapely figure well modeled by a snug dark-red jersey dress which nearly matched the well-coifed hair.

She gave him a lazy, slightly lascivious smile of welcome, her torso leaning forward slightly, the wide-spread arms supported on the counter by the heels of her hands.

"Well, Mr. Fenner," she said with mock formality. "What can we do for you this afternoon?"

"I could use a little help."

"That's what we're here for."

Fenner took Valano's four-by-fives from his pocket and selected two prints. He knew she was watching him but he purposely made her wait.

"Yesterday you said you'd noticed a man walk across the street Saturday. You thought he turned into this building. You said he was dreamy, or something like that. You looked him right in the eye but he wouldn't give you a tumble. Remember?"

"Sure I remember."

"He got out of a gray sports car, probably foreign."

"Right." The green eyes were watchful now, her curiosity aroused. "What about it?"

Fenner showed her the two photographs, one full face, the other a partial profile. "Is this dreamboat?"

"It sure is," she said, very positive and nodding vigorously. "Don't you think he's cute? Do you know him?"

"I know him," Fenner said, and laughed at her reaction.

"What's his name?"

"I can't tell you that. Not yet anyway."

"Oh, great!" she said with simulated disgust. "You ask the questions but you hold out the answers."

"He's not very good material anyway, Marge."

"Why not?"

"For one thing, he's married."

She considered this and batted her mascaraed lids, her look bold but mischievous.

"So?"

"He also pays the rent for a girl a bit younger and sexier than his wife. I don't think he'd be on the market for anything more just now; he's got too much on his plate already."

She shrugged, accepting the news with a small grimace. Fenner understood how it was with Marge. That she had tried marriage and found it unsatisfactory in some respects had by no means discouraged her. She very clearly believed in the institution itself. She could be said to be available. But not in the area of one-night stands unless her partner was a likely prospect for a more permanent and legal liaison, or unless there was some good reason for a trial run. She was, however, philosophical about this recent and disappointing bit of news.

"That's my kind of luck all right. . . . Say!" The eyes opened again, her flirtation forgotten. "You think this guy knows something about those murders upstairs?"

"I really don't know." Fenner kept his tone casually evasive. "But young Lipscomb hired me to do what I can to help find his father's killer. I have to check every possibility, no matter how remote it may seem."

As he spoke it occurred to him he really would have liked to ask Marge out for drinks and dinner by way of repayment. The truth was, he was afraid to. For this was an attractive woman with a lot going for her. She was also a bit aggressive and quite possibly possessive. To take a chance when his present situation was so satisfactory could mean an unwanted involvement and he knew it. To change the subject he retrieved his prints and said:

"The charter boys in?"

"Yeah," she said with studied disinterest. "How about that? Both of them. . . . But," she added as Fenner started to turn away, "we have much more glamorous trips—special rates for two, you know?"

Fenner said he knew, and walked past the graying Miss Asnip, who gave him a cold and disapproving eye. The unctuous Mr. Harris, like an unprepared schoolboy afraid he would be called on to recite, at once began to shuffle papers when he realized Fenner was headed his way. But Fenner went by him, continuing to the closed door at the end. He knocked firmly. When someone in the room answered with a growling sound that was otherwise inarticulate, he opened the door and stepped inside.

The growl apparently came from Max Coburn because Charlie Hyatt was leaning well back in his chair, crossed heels on one corner of his desk, a telephone cradled against one ear while he made some notes on a pad.

Hyatt, he knew, was the businessman and looked it—a pin-striped flannel in medium gray, blue shirt, conservative tie, expensive-looking black loafers with tassels. His job was not only to line up the planes used for gambling charters but also to solicit customers whose credit rating and net worth had been carefully checked beforehand.

Before the two had set up the operation with the blessing and initial financing of the district syndicate heads, Max Coburn had been a freelance enforcer for certain moneylenders since he had the requisite skills for inflicting painful but nonfatal injuries on recalcitrant debtors. Because of his build and his menacing facial expression such force was seldom necessary in the present operation; in addition, his voice on the telephone calling a man, his wife, or relatives was both anonymous and frightening.

Perhaps no more than six feet tall, he weighed close to two hundred, with a washboard stomach and a muscular thickness across the chest and shoulders. That, plus a blocky face and black eyes deepset under bushy brows that nearly met over the bridge of his nose, only added to his effectiveness, especially when he scowled. Actually he was basically a genial character when he wasn't working. He dressed in loud clothes, his idea of sartorial splendor being plaid jackets in various hues, checked slacks, and wildly colorful open-necked sport shirts.

Fenner, half listening to Hyatt's bargaining, lit a cigarette and said, "How's business, Max?"

Coburn stuck a cigar in his mouth and spoke past it. "Fantastic. Just filled a charter with the parishioners at St. Agnes's."

Fenner grunted, his squint at once skeptical. "You're kidding."

"Nope."

"They're not putting up a grand apiece, for God's sake?"

"Three fifty."

"To where, Niagara Falls?"

"The Bahamas. Freeport."

"Chips?"

"Twenty bucks a head. Of course the wives—lots of wives goin'—want to play the slots, that's cash. And some dames you wouldn't believe once they get cranking that handle."

"Where's your profit?" Fenner said, sitting down.

"There ain't none. I mean, there could be a little but we don't count on it. Good will," Max said proudly. "Charlie convinced the man it's good advertising. These sharp young executive and professional types that got some kind of credit and want to get away from the wife and kids for what they figure can be a free weekend, you show 'em this St. Agnes deal with the blessing of the priest, they're convinced we're legit—and we are. Ain't we?"

Hyatt, who had rung off and heard the last sentence, said, "What we don't need is guys like you, Jack."

Fenner blew smoke and suppressed a grin.

"You checked out my credit."

"Credit's fine."

"Everything compted." Coburn removed the cigar and frowned at the ash. "Dinners, shows, drinks. Seven Cs in chips. And what do you do all day?"

"Plays golf," Hyatt said, half laughing.

"Even takes his sticks and shoes with him."

"And gets off at Logan," Hyatt finished, "with what was it, four Cs?" He watched Fenner nod, glanced at Coburn, and winked. "But we could have just the thing for you. Aruba."

"Yeah." Coburn growled. "No golf 's far as I know."

"How does Curaçao or Bonaire sound?" Hyatt said. "You know Dutch? We're even dickering with Surinam. Paramaribo. You know, South America. First charter ever, we hope. Hell of a selling point."

"Also no golf, they tell us," Coburn growled. "Never even heard of the game. Down there you gotta gamble or flip. No guarantees on gash either except local."

Fenner just sat there, green eyes amused as the pair ran out of conversation. He knew that once they stopped their good-natured banter there would be questions. They had a neat and profitable business and it constantly amazed him how easy it was to sell doctors, dentists, advertising men, sales executives into putting up a thousand or twelve hundred for what promised to be a cheap and glamorous weekend. After all, each customer got seven or eight hundred in chips free. He didn't have to gamble, did he? He could cash them in, couldn't he?

Of course some were older men who wanted to gamble and could afford it and didn't need convincing. But the majority always seemed to be younger, moderately successful, with split-levels in Needham or Hingham or Weston, two cars, often a boat. And when they came back, having signed nearly forgotten casino markers with the pit-bosses, many in shock at what they owed, Coburn saw to it they paid off promptly or handed over a weekly interest payment they could not afford for long. Somehow most managed to settle the original debt. If they didn't have stocks and bonds to sell, there was always a second mortgage to be had, or insurance on which a loan could be arranged, or a forced sale of the boat. . . .

"What?" Fenner said, rousing himself and trying to concentrate.

"I said, this just a social call?" Hyatt said, a touch of suspicion shading his tone.

"Or," said Coburn, his cigar forgotten, "does it have something to do with that hit upstairs?"

Their interest aroused by this new subject, they took alternate lines like two stand-up comics, and for a few sentences Fenner needed no reply.

"You didn't know the guy?" Hyatt asked.

"He sure as hell wasn't local."

"Why'd he pick your office?"

"Or did somebody pick it for him?"

"The cops identify him yet?"

"They got a theory?"

"Two in the back of the head sounds like it was a pro."

"But small caliber, I heard."

"Could be a reason for that," Hyatt said.

Fenner broke in on the dialogue. He told them Ludlow had been identified by the local, New York, and Washington authorities. He gave Ludlow's New York address, adding that he had come from Cincinnati and was apparently an odd-job and small-time bag man, runner, and courier with mob connections.

"What was he doin' in town then?" Coburn asked.

"I think he brought something with him."

"Like what?" Hyatt said.

"Like maybe four hundred thousand in stock certificates, probably hot."

Hyatt, still thinking, swung his heels off the desk. "Nobody *gives* even hot stock away," he said. "If he brought it he must have expected something in exchange. What?"

"That," said Fenner, "is what I'm hoping to find out." He pulled his legs in and sat up, gaze narrowing and his tone demanding. "I told you what I know; now you tell me what you know about a guy named Bruce Townsend. I understand he took a trip with you."

"One," Hyatt said.

"To where?"

"Vegas."

"What did he drop?"

"Six and a half."

"Large?"

"Large."

Fenner looked at Coburn, who had finally discarded his dead cigar. "How long did he pay the vig?"

"Two weeks."

"No trouble?"

"Just the usual squawk. When he saw how it was he came up with what he owed and got his markers back like a little gentleman. Trouble is, he ain't been back. Cards, dice, roulette're not his bag."

"I heard football," Fenner said.

"You heard right," Hyatt said. "Has a lot of action in the season. A dozen bets a week, maybe half college, half pro. Whenever he thinks he spots an overlay."

"How's he been doing on the average?"

"Wins some, loses some. Probably winds up dropping maybe two or three a year. Nothing big."

"Except once," Fenner said. "I hear he went overboard on last year's Super Bowl. Big enough so nobody in town would cover it but Maurie Matlock."

"I think you heard right again," Coburn said. "Townsend went for thirty, the stupid bastard. Thinks he's got the overlay of the year."

"Because," Hyatt added, "he played some quarterback for Harvard. Not so hot with the pass but a great scrambler. And Tarkenton's a scrambler. And Townsend figures with Minnesota's line, and Tarkenton wearing the Dolphins' linemen out chasing him, the Vikings're in. So he takes them and six. . . . Some overlay," he added disgustedly. "You know what happened?"

"Miami takes the kickoff and works it straight down and over for seven," Fenner said.

"And the Vikings receive and can't move and have to punt. So what happens? Same thing. Down the field again to make it fourteen and they never give up the ball. The crowd could have gone home then: 24–7, wasn't it, the final?"

"Max . . ." Fenner waited until he had Coburn's attention. "What would be the weekly vigorish on thirty?"

"Depends on how many points Matlock wants. A guy like

Townsend, his old man practically dead and some inheritance coming in, Matlock might settle for twelve Cs on the thirty. They tell me Townsend still owes the thirty. Now and then he pays the vig; when he don't Matlock lets him sign another marker. Christ knows how much Townsend'll need to clear the books. . . . I think," he added half to himself, "unless the old man kicks off pretty soon Maurie'll get most of young Townsend's cut of the estate, is what I think."

Fenner had watched the frown biting into Hyatt's brow and now, eyes half open, Hyatt said, "Just what's your interest in Townsend, Jack? You figure he could know something about that upstairs thing?"

Fenner, who had been expecting some such question, stood up and shrugged off an answer. "Hell no, not directly. Only, Townsend is carrying a heavy load, and he's in the stock and bond business. In my racket you got to start somewhere. You get all you can, anywhere you can, and see if anything adds up. Which sometimes it does. . . . When you two line up a charter to somewhere like say, Pebble Beach—"

"Get out of here," Max growled good-naturedly. "You're wasting our time."

About to open the door, Fenner turned back and asked if he could use the telephone. Among the thoughts that had come to him that day, and the tentative schedule he had mapped out for himself, was a call at the Townsend home in Brookline. He knew the odds were against his gaining an interview, but experience told him that there were times when the odds had to be ignored. Now as Hyatt nodded and pushed one of the telephones on the desk to one corner, Fenner added that he would need a directory.

Hyatt swiveled his chair and produced one from a shelf behind him. Aware that the pair were eyeing him curiously, but not caring, Fenner found his number. As he dialed he wondered just what he could say.

After three rings a pleasant feminine voice said, "Paton

Townsend's residence," and Fenner wondered if this was the latest in a succession of nurse-housekeepers who had worked for the old man since his third wife had been killed at Myopia Hunt riding to the hounds many years earlier.

"This is Mr. Fenner, Jack Fenner," he said. "I did some work for one of Mr. Townsend's sons a while back and I wondered if it would be possible for me to come out and see him for a few minutes."

There were some seconds of silence, during which he crossed mental fingers; then he got a break. For once the speaker was identified he realized he might get more understanding than could be expected from a strange housekeeper.

"Yes, Mr. Fenner. I think we met once and Alan told me quite a lot about you when you helped on his divorce. This is Caroline Townsend, Bruce's wife. I came out to lunch with Paton and—" She broke off and tried again. "Are you aware of his condition?"

"I know it's serious. Emphysema, isn't it?"

"He has great difficulty breathing. Even more so when he talks. I—I really don't know. Could you tell me what it's about?"

Fenner was floundering and he knew it. He also knew why. To call on Paton Townsend would be little more than a fishing expedition, an awkward attempt to add some bits and pieces of information to the few facts he had.

"Well," he said finally, "it's about your husband. I know he's heavily in debt to a local gambler and has been for some time. I wondered if Mr. Townsend could help me find out just how much trouble Bruce is in." He paused again, feeling the perspiration on his forehead. Then, as a new thought came to him, he snared it and said, "You could help if you can spare the time. I mean, you could sort of talk for him. I promise not to stay long."

"Well—"

"Would you ask him?"

Jack Fenner had admired Caroline Townsend's well-bred

attractiveness for a long time, though he had only met her once and that briefly. What she said then served only to enhance that admiration.

"If it's really important," she said, her tone abruptly warm and almost conspiratorial, "why don't you just come? I'll explain the situation. Once Paton knows you're on your way he'll be too well-mannered to refuse to see you." She laughed lightly. "Oh, he may grumble a bit, but only at me. . . . How long will you be?"

Fenner said fifteen or twenty minutes and when he rang off he was unwilling to meet the charter boys' inquisitive stares. He mumbled his thanks and left, not looking back.

13

THE TOWNSEND HOME in the Brookline district stood perhaps a hundred feet back from a quiet street. Protected from curious eyes by a six-foot, neatly trimmed hedge with two openings for the semicircular drive, it was designed with an antique-brick, three-story main structure flanked by balanced two-story wings of white-painted clapboard. A BMW Bavaria stood opposite the front steps, and as Fenner parked behind it he was reminded of Bruce Townsend's Mercedes, deciding this was a foreign-car family.

A chime sounded somewhere deep inside the house when he pushed the button, ignoring the massive antique metal knocker on the heavy white-painted door. After perhaps five seconds it opened and Caroline Townsend's gray eyes took a quick, appraising, all-inclusive look at him before she offered a small smile and stepped back.

She was tall for a woman, about five-nine in medium heels, with a full but supple figure that moved with some inbred poise and grace. The dark-blond hair, worn shorter than most, was thick and lustrous. The wide, generous mouth was quick to smile, there was no artfulness in her manner, and there was an undeniable physical attractiveness that Fenner found highly appealing.

"Hello, Mr. Fenner," she said, and offered a hand that was as soft as her grip was firm. "Come in."

She moved away to let him close the door and then he was following her into a wide hall with openings on the right and left. A gracefully designed staircase mounted straight ahead and curved back near the top to the second-floor landing. He had a glimpse of a dim, book-lined study on his right and then he was moving across a long living room with wide-board floors and orientals and heavy, expensive-looking furniture that appeared in the half-light to be little used.

The room beyond in the left wing where the woman led him would probably have been called a conservatory or sunroom in other days. One wall was all windows and French doors. Opposite was a natural stone fireplace with an opening large enough to hide an upright piano, and a long, one-piece granite mantle. The furniture was bright and chintzy, the one anachronism a modern padded armchair that could be tilted in various positions.

Nearby was a Bennett respirator that looked as if it belonged in a hospital. A metal column was supported by a four-branch base on casters for easy movement. The top was a box with a glassed-in white panel and three or four dials. From the bottom a cablelike connection was plugged into a wall socket, similar to an electric outlet. A fatter, transparent tube led from the bottom of the box to Paton Townsend. Flexible, with a small, liquid-filled cylinder attached to the underside, it ended in a rubber and plastic mask, at the moment held to the man's mouth and nose but with an elastic headband for more permanent positioning.

Fenner, uncertain as to just what he could expect, was shocked by the older man's appearance. Not a big man but always vital and athletic-looking, he had been well known locally as a competent practitioner of such society sports as golf, polo, sculling, and, in the winter, curling. The once-handsome face was much thinner, the color odd, but it was the unexpected deformity of the chest area that surprised Fenner. Alan Townsend had told him a year ago that his father might live two more years; one of these had been used. Prepared to find a flat-chested, desiccated figure, Fenner now saw that the chest had been expanded somehow from within to become abnormally thick and rounded from front to back.

He tried to recall what he had read about the condition. The blocking off, or filling, of the capillaries or smaller branches of the lungs had spread toward the center, which had to expand to compensate for the failure of the tributaries. No longer elastic or workable, the failure of the organs to function made it more difficult, and finally impossible, to exhale and expel any air at all. At least that was Fenner's half-baked understanding.

Such thoughts took but seconds and Fenner was at once aware of the bright and burning eyes that watched him above the mask. Townsend was waiting. So was Caroline, and Fenner said:

"You won't have to talk much, Mr. Townsend. I appreciate your seeing me and I'd like to tell you what happened to me in the last two days—in case you missed the item in the papers."

Townsend nodded and, somewhat unexpectedly, held out his right hand. Fenner took it and found the handshake hot and bony but still firm. Townsend motioned the woman to the divan and indicated a closer chair for Fenner, then nodded, indicating Fenner was to continue.

Fenner obeyed, his angular face somber, avoiding Townsend's steady gaze. He had already decided on his opening remarks. Still not knowing quite what he could prove but stubborn about it, he began his story with his weekend and concluded with the discovery of the murder in his office and the one across the hall. Without going into any detail he spoke of Leslie Ludlow and his own guess as to why Ludlow had come up from New York and what he had brought with him.

By then he could almost do this by rote and as he talked his mind reviewed what he knew about the family. The Townsend men, it seemed, did not have a very good track record in the marital department. Paton's first wife, Alan's mother, had been unfortunate enough to get pneumonia before the discovery and use of antibiotics and miracle drugs. Paton had hired a nurse-governess for the boy and married again two or three years later. This wife, Bruce's mother, had been killed not too long after his birth when, driving back from a party in Duxbury one rainy Sunday night with a male companion, the car failed to make a curve on the slick, crowned macadam.

The third marriage some years later had been to a much younger woman, a vivacious brunette from a good family. The daughter, now in Florence, had been born of this union and that marriage, a happy one so far as Fenner knew, had lasted the longest. Alan had started college and Bruce was in prep school when the accident at Myopia Hunt had snuffed out her life. Since then there had been a succession of housekeepers, all handsome, robust women in the lower ranges of middle age, and it was said that they served in capacities other than those usually called for. Apparently such liaisons were mutually satisfactory since they all left amicably, with generous severance settlements. . . .

He sensed he was coming to the end of his account and tried to forecast Townsend's reaction when he finished. Fatally ill as he was, the man's eyes were alive and attentive and his first remark held no surprise.

Lowering the mask, he coughed to clear the vaporized oxygen from his throat and spoke, his voice husky, labored, but clearly understandable.

"Caroline told me your visit concerned my son Bruce. In what way?"

Fenner knew that in the end he was going to tell Townsend what he knew of Bruce's whereabouts on Saturday morning but there were things he wanted to know first.

"In several ways, Mr. Townsend," he said, taking pains with his words. "But first I'd like to ask if you know about your son's debt to a man named Matlock."

"I know he's in debt up to his ears. I never ask who to."

"Has he come to you for financial help?"

"He did some months ago. I told him no." He used the mask for a minute or so, removed it, coughed again. "I told him I'd helped him all I was going to. I paid off two girls, one while he was in college and one a year or so after he graduated. I thought when he married Caroline he'd grow up."

Fenner glanced at the woman who was watching her father-in-law, the gray eyes soft with sympathy and understanding.

"He did, Paton," she said quietly. "He really did. Oh, I knew he gambled some on football games in the fall but never very much."

"He was a damn fine athlete," Townsend said, as though the previous subject had been forgotten. "He'd have been first string at Harvard except for the bad luck of being in the same class with an all-Ivy quarterback who could pass better. . . . You know what he did to keep in shape? Played lacrosse in the spring. If you really want to get bashed around week after week, not counting practice, that's the game."

He tried the mask again, his gaze narrowed in thought. "He was my favorite, damn him," he said when he could. "Maybe because he could take it. I was never a spare-the-rod father. Until they were twelve, the boys anyway, they got a damn good spanking when they got out of line or disobeyed me more than once.

"Alan was different," he said weakly. "One spanking was enough. He learned his lesson quickly, never gave me any trouble; was well mannered and considerate and a damn sight smarter." He paused as if gathering strength. "Bruce always had a defiant, don't-give-a-damn attitude. He'd risk another spanking, gambling he could get away with things, just like he gambled on football games later. He was always the more likable somehow, more demonstrative.

"When he came and told me about that idiotic thirty thousand bet I think he expected I'd bail him out," he added in fury and despair. "I told him no. His mother left him some money in trust; he's to get it when he's thirty-five—that's four years—and he wanted me to invade the capital. When they put me in a box he can have it; not before. He gets the interest the fund earns and that's all."

Again he used the mask and Fenner glanced at Caroline, seeing the worry and compassion in the smooth, well-boned face. She had none of Laura Latimer's blatant sexuality but he had an idea she could be a warm and passionate partner to any man she loved. She seemed not to be aware of him in her concern, and presently Townsend was coughing again preparatory to speaking.

"How much would the interest be on thirty thousand? What is it they call it?"

"Vigorish."

"Yes, vigorish. How much?"

"I understand in his case twelve hundred a week."

"Good God!" Townsend shook his head in wonderment.

"If you don't pay on time you sign another marker and they add it to the original debt."

"Then if you let it mount to, say, fifty—" Townsend tried again. "You mean that he would owe two thousand a week just for interest . . ." The words trailed off and he shifted his weight, seeking some comfort. "They haven't hurt him, have they?" he said, digressing in some sudden anxiety.

"Not that I know of."

"I've read of gamblers found with broken bones, and in cars and vacant lots, with bullets in their heads."

"I don't think that will happen just yet," Fenner said.

"Why not?"

"Because they know about you and your condition, probably about the trust fund. They have ways of checking pretty thoroughly."

"Twelve hundred a week, maybe two thousand," Townsend said as though finding the thought abhorrent. "And he still owes thirty. Have you any idea what the total is now?" He watched Fenner shake his head. "Where's he going to get it?

"Forty a year in salary," he continued, not expecting an

answer. "What few investments he had long gone. His mother's trust brings him another fifteen plus. Business the way it's been he'll be lucky to get ten from his minor interest in the firm this year. On top of that he's paying rent and God knows what else for that chippie from New York. That model-actress-tart—"

"*Dad!*"

Caroline, seeing the old man struggling to express himself, spoke with uncommon sharpness. She rose, moved to his chair and adjusted his oxygen mask.

"You rest," she commanded. "Let me do the talking for a while. I know the story. Just remember you can't blame that woman for Bruce's crazy football bet. That happened long before he even met her and you know it."

She went back to the divan and sat down, her folded hands coming to rest on one knee as the gray eyes met Fenner's curious gaze. Before she could speak he said:

"Did he ask you for help?"

"No." She shook her head. "Probably because he realized I couldn't help in any worthwhile way. My father set up a trust with the bank for me too. I can live comfortably on it but there's seldom more than a few thousand in my checking account. Since Bruce moved out I've had to assume expenses that normally would be his. There isn't a great deal left. Frankly," she said, not looking at Townsend, "I think Paton should have given Bruce the money. It would have been his some day anyway."

Townsend sat up a few inches, tore off the mask in his eagerness to repudiate such heresy. His necessary coughing stopped him for a few seconds so that when he could speak there was no anger in his tone, only determination.

"Bruce hasn't been gambling recently. I've asked around."

"I know," she said calmly. "But maybe his mistress should get credit for that."

"If I'd paid off that loss he would have kept right at it," Townsend said, ignoring the comment. "This could be one hell of an expensive lesson but maybe it will be worth it once he gets away from that woman. Thank God," he said to Fenner, "Caroline's the kind who can understand and forgive. She knows he'll come back and she loves the idiot enough to wait. You do still love him, don't you?"

"You know I do," the woman said without embarrassment.

The room was quiet then and Fenner waited, sensing somehow that Townsend's mind was working and that he would come presently to other questions that had to be answered. He could see the change coming in the man's face, the narrowing of the eyes above the mask, the suspicion growing. Deliberately then the mask came off, the coughing somehow suppressed.

"This trouble you spoke of when you talked to Caroline. It was something more than my son's gambling mess, wasn't it?"

"Possibly." Fenner's tone was quiet but direct. "I have a witness who says your son was outside my office building Saturday morning somewhere around the time those two murders took place upstairs. The witness isn't positive Bruce actually went inside but he was headed that way. She didn't see him leave but she saw him get out of his car and cross the street."

Fenner, half expecting an angry and vehement argument or a flat denial, was surprised at Townsend's reaction. There was somehow a studied challenge in the weak and raspy voice.

"Have you been to the police with this information?"

"No."

"Why not?"

"For one reason, it would be the witness's word against his, provided he can prove an alibi. For another, I'm no longer a sworn officer of the law. I know your son and I'm at least a casual friend of Alan's. I can't run the risk of being charged with obstructing justice, but I try to avoid implicating an innocent person or subjecting him to intensive police interrogation on unsubstantiated evidence.

"I've been retained," he continued in the same level tones,

"to find out who killed Mr. Lipscomb. I intend to do what I can to help the investigation. Four strangers were seen entering that building Saturday morning. The victim was one; your son was another."

"Have you talked to Bruce about this?" Townsend said tiredly.

"No, but I intend to." Fenner stood up. "I wanted to see if you knew how seriously he was involved in that gambling debt and how much he owed."

Townsend seemed to be considering the remark and then he came to a point Fenner had hoped would not be mentioned.

"I understand that much," he said. "What I don't understand is that so far I haven't heard any explanation or even a reasonable theory that would give Bruce a motive to kill this man Ludlow. Why? How did he know the fellow if he's from New York? What did he want with Bruce?"

"I'm afraid I can't answer those questions. I do have a thought," Fenner said. "I have a hunch that Ludlow was carrying those markers of Bruce's as proof of his indebtedness. Just what Ludlow expected to trade them for I can't say."

To himself he added, *at least I'm not about to,* and he was relieved when Townsend did not press the point. Instead he seemed to be looking beyond Fenner at something that had no part of the room. When he finally spoke it became obvious that his mind had moved on to what for him was more important.

"When you see Bruce tell him this. I've got one year left, hopefully, and I'm not volunteering to cut it short. Bruce will just have to wait until they put me in a box before he can collect on that trust. But while I'm alive I'll spend every dollar I have to prove his innocence. He never killed anyone no matter what your witness says."

Fenner nodded and said he understood. But in his mind he remembered other parents, particularly mothers, even when a son had been caught red-handed after some vicious crime, proclaiming in tearful tones that her boy could not be guilty;

he had always been a good boy; he could not have done such a thing.

Caroline Townsend was beside him then, and at a nod, he followed her from the room. At the front door he said he was sorry if he had upset her father-in-law and hoped she would forgive the intrusion.

She managed a small smile. Her manner remained as gracious as her voice.

"At least he knows the truth. He could even change his mind after he's thought about it. He gets so bored sitting around day after day, breathing vapor piped up from those oxygen tanks in the cellar. That's why I try to get out here two or three times a week. . . . I'm really awfully glad you came," she added, offering her hand. "I know it's hard for him to talk but I think it's good for him to get worked up and excited about things once in a while, a chance to blow off steam. And he still loves Bruce, no matter what he says."

"Just as you do."

"Oh, yes." She smiled wistfully. "But in a somewhat different way. Also I have more patience than Paton. And he *is* right about one thing you know. Bruce didn't kill those men. He couldn't even have known them; how could he?"

She expected no answer and Fenner supplied none as he went down the steps. Instead he asked himself a silent question. How could any man in his right mind walk away from a woman who had so much to offer and seemed so willing to give? The answer was obvious. Bruce Townsend's current affair had affected both his mind *and* his judgment.

14

THE APARTMENT was in the Kenmore district, a five-story brick-and-stone building already showing its age. The interior had been laid out in three-, four-, and five-room apartments for those unable or unwilling to pay for all the modern luxuries or a more fashionable neighborhood. With Bruce Townsend's continuing financial burdens, Fenner could well understand the man's inability to afford something better for his mistress.

It was nearly five now and Fenner had been parked diagonally across the street for nearly an hour. In recent years he usually assigned routine stakeouts to others in the business whose hourly rates were more reasonable, but in this instance the job demanded his personal attention. He had examined the apartment entrance soon after parking. There was no marquee, no doorman. But the outer and inner glass doors were locked, so there was nothing to do but sit as patiently as possible and wait for a break. With any kind of luck Laura Latimer should be arriving from work shortly—by cab or escorted by Bruce Townsend. Either way Fenner intended to be invited inside.

Hardly more than ten minutes later it happened the way he hoped it would. A taxi, coming from the right direction, angled toward the curb and stopped opposite the entrance. While

Laura Latimer was paying the driver Fenner was crossing the pavement. She had reached the door and was searching for her keys when he hailed her.

"Miss Latimer?"

She wheeled, keys in hand. She wore a smart, brown tweed suit with a white blouse, and the pulled-back black hair seemed an appropriate style for a successful young business-woman. After her first startled glance recognition came, and with it her smile.

"Mr. Fenner—well." The smile remained tentative, uncer-tain. "Were you waiting for me?"

Fenner gave her back her smile, the soul of geniality, a man without a care in the world.

"To tell the truth," he lied cheerfully, intent on being thoroughly convincing, "I was hoping to catch Bruce. I phoned his club," he added, compounding the lie since he had done no such thing, "and they told me he might be here."

"He will be shortly," she said in her Southern, actor's-school accent. She unlocked the door and he stood behind her as she did the same thing with the inner door. "So come on up. You can make us a drink while we wait for him."

The living room of the small third-floor apartment had a furnished, ordinary, and well-used look, the chairs and sofa early chainstore, the coffee table and occasional pieces ve-neered maple and tacky-looking. The wall-to-wall carpet showed much wear in spots and the lamp shades needed replacing. Altogether it was not a place Bruce Townsend would have picked had his financial obligations been lighter.

She had already shrugged out of her jacket by the time Fenner had closed the door, and now she pointed toward the dinette and the swinging kitchen door beyond.

"I'm feeding Bruce here tonight," she said, "believe it or not. Will you do the honors while I get out of my business uniform? You may have to pry some ice out of a tray. Whisky in the cabinet above. Scotch-on-the-rocks for me, please . . .

I'll only be a minute," she added, and disappeared down a small hallway to the right.

Jack Fenner, quite pleased with his subterfuge since it was the woman he had wanted to talk to all the time, had the drinks ready and was sitting on the sofa when she reappeared five minutes later, and the change in her appearance was startling and complete. The pale-blue knit slacks fitted snugly but not indecently and proved that her legs were straight, perhaps a touch thick in the thigh but not flabby. Her waist was flat in the front and the hips and bottom shapely and well proportioned. The white jersey turtleneck was sufficiently revealing to suggest breasts that were not only adequate but firmly formed.

What completed the transformation was her hair. No longer trapped in her parted and pulled-back workaday style, it fell thickly to curl upward at the ends just as it touched her shoulders. This, the smooth olive skin, the arched brows and the skillful touch of lipstick to widen the small mouth gave her a look that was wholly feminine and sexually desirable; a bit predatory perhaps but not too bold.

Fenner stood as she approached and handed her her drink. She said, "Thanks. I see you found everything." Motioning him back to his seat, she curled at one end of the sofa, one foot and leg tucked gracefully under her.

She said, "Cheers," and Fenner said, "Cheers," and she said, "Well, how's the murder investigation going?"

"Slowly," Fenner said, and then, knowing he would get a rise out of her and wanting one, he added, "I was out to Paton Townsend's this afternoon. Caroline was there."

"Oh, oh," she said; then, voice flattening, "I'll bet they gave you an earful about little Laura. That old man would love to wring my neck."

She took a sip of her drink, her mouth twisting at one corner, a sleepy, faraway look in her dark eyes. "All about how the ex-waitress, model, and would-be actress got Bruce up to her hotel room one night and seduced him while his faithful, devoted, society-type wife waited for her dissolute and wandering husband."

Fenner waited, his only response a shrug.

"Well, didn't they?" she pressed, her annoyance showing.

"Paton started to sound off. Caroline stopped him. She didn't say much of anything about you or your affair. I think she still loves him."

"Oh, sure." With some contempt. "And if she waits Bruce will come back like a naughty boy and everything will be all right again." She made a small, throaty sound that seemed uncomplimentary. "Well, she's got one hell of a long wait," she added bluntly. "Bruce was completely honest with her once he made up his mind. He asked for a divorce. It's not his fault if she won't cooperate."

She took more of her drink and her dark gaze came back to him, her frown digging little wrinkles in her brow.

"You know how it started, don't you?"

"All I heard," Fenner said, "was how Bruce was invited to sit in on rehearsals by some friend who had put some money in the production."

"That's exactly how it happened. He'd never had anything to do with the theater before and he was fascinated by the whole routine. He was at rehearsal every morning. He never missed a performance during the week we lasted. Once we'd met he was waiting for me after the curtain every night. And when I saw how he felt I was honest with him too. I told him where I'd come from and how I'd had some parts in high school plays. I wasn't another poor little girl from the wrong side of the tracks whose father beat her or tried to rape her. I left because life at home was unbearably dull, and neither my father nor my mother cared particularly what I did; there just wasn't any love or affection in the house.

"I had a few hundred saved," she said, "and I tried the modeling agencies. I wasn't tall enough or flat enough—" she glanced down with some approval at her breasts—"for high fashion or any kind of fashion. What I got was a job as a waitress. On the West Side, and some garment manufacturers used to come in for lunch and one day I was offered a job. Sometimes dresses, Junior Miss size; sometimes underwear."

She put her empty glass down but shook her head when Fenner started to get a refill. She wasn't looking at him now. Stubbornness showed in her mouth and chin and her gaze seemed focused inward.

"Four or five times a year I had to entertain important out-of-town buyers. The bosses left me alone once I made it clear how it had to be but the buyers, well, that was different somehow. An expensive dinner, a night on the town pub-crawling. What the hell, I wasn't a virgin when I left home.

"You only lose it once, don't you?" she asked rhetorically. "And the extra money helped with my acting lessons. I got into a few off-Broadway-type productions, none of them too successful, and then my big break came. At least that's what I told myself," she added, her mouth dipping still more.

"It was a turkey from the beginning but I was too dumb, or maybe too anxious to know it. All those rehearsals in New York and stumbling through a week here; new scenes every day, the reviewers panning us. The only good thing was Bruce. We threw one of those celebration-in-reverse parties the Saturday night we closed. Everyone got tight and when Bruce took me back to my hotel he wanted to come up and I thought why not? He was a sweet guy, not like anyone I'd ever known. I guess I was half in love with him by that time anyway even though I knew he was married. I thought, give the poor guy a good time, Laura, and then go back to the grind.

"So I did," she said. "And the next weekend he appeared in New York. And except for dinner and a couple of nightclubs we spent a lot of time in his hotel suite. The next week the same, only this time he said he thought he had a job for me; he'd scouted around for an apartment and he thought he'd found one. Not swanky but it would do until his divorce came through. So I came. And I'm glad I did," she said defiantly. "If

Caroline can wait, so can I. What I have with Bruce is worth waiting for. For appearance's sake he has his club for an address. When he wants to spend the night here he does. We're not hiding anything from anyone."

• She lapsed into silence then and Fenner let it continue until he thought she would be able to answer some questions without resentment. What he had heard and what he had seen in the past few minutes told him that this was a worldly, selfish, and determined woman, seldom bothered by any great concern for others. He also knew somehow that, unencumbered, sitting close to her on a banquette in some nightclub, thigh against thigh, he might have a problem.

"Laura," he said finally, using her given name for the first time. When her gaze came back to him, he said, "Do you know the spot Bruce is in with a local gambler? He's in pretty heavy. His father doesn't see how he can pay the weekly interest on his present income, and he isn't even contributing to his wife's support. If she took him into court—"

"She has enough." There was a surliness in the tone now.

"So have a lot of women. That doesn't stop them from prosecuting the husband. . . . Have you any idea how much he's in the hole?"

"No. I know it's a lot but when I ask him he says not to worry, that he can handle it. I don't see how it's any of your business but if you really want to know why don't you ask him?"

As though Bruce Townsend had been waiting for his cue, a key scratched in the lock. As the door swung open Townsend came in, a brown sack of groceries under one arm and a look of complete surprise on his handsome face. For a long moment he simply stood there glancing from one to the other; then, the momentary frown turning into a cautious smile, he advanced.

"Hey, Jack."

Before he could continue or Fenner reply Laura said hurriedly, "He's been waiting for you. They told him at the club you might be here and he was waiting outside and I asked him up for a drink."

"Swell." Townsend bent to kiss her soundly, juggling the bag before heading for the kitchen. "I'll join you. Come on, Jack. You two need refills; you can help."

Once in the small kitchen, the door swinging behind them, Townsend put the bag down and his frown came back, a look of puzzlement in the blue eyes.

"Anything special, Jack?" he asked as he dropped cubes in the glasses.

"I was out to see your father this afternoon. Caroline was there. We had a talk."

"Oh? About what?"

"About the spot you're in with Maurie Matlock for one thing."

"And how would you know about that?" Townsend was pouring now, his tone coolly indifferent.

"Rumors mostly. Every gambler in town has probably heard about that old Super Bowl game and what you went for. So after what happened in my office yesterday morning I've been asking some questions. The word is you still owe the thirty plus God knows how much vigorish by now. You went to your father for the thirty," he said, and went on to give the gist of his earlier conversation.

Having finished pouring the drinks, Townsend handed Fenner his glass and elbowed his way through the swinging door with the other two. When he had delivered them he sat down beside Laura and slid an arm lightly about her shoulders. When he was ready he gave Fenner a challenging, slightly resentful look.

"And is that why you came? To find out what the present total is?"

"Not entirely." Fenner took a swallow, put down the glass, and took from his inside pocket a photocopy of the list of securities he had found in Ludlow's suit at the Starlight Motel.

"You've seen this. You helped figure the total."

"So?"

"Lieutenant Bacon down at homicide has a copy of this and he hasn't rejected my thought that Ludlow came up from New York with the certificates represented on that list. If I'm right Ludlow must either have brought them to make delivery or to exchange them.

"I had a long talk with Fred Sampson at the *Courier*," he added. "I showed him the list and we got talking about the series of losses suffered by New York banks and brokerage houses the past two or three years, some of them officially undisclosed to prevent unwanted publicity."

He spoke of the recent three million plus rip-off in New York and asked if Townsend knew the difference between hot and cold stocks. When he got a nod, he said:

"I wonder if you'd check your own vault or your microfilm records to see if that list could be duplicated by certificates that you have in your inventory."

Townsend put his glass down on the coffee table with care He removed his arm from the woman's shoulder. His mouth had a noticeable stiffness now and when he spoke his voice was coldly resentful, like his eyes.

"Go on. What's the rest of it?"

"There isn't any." Fenner tried to sound casual and it took some effort. "I asked Fred Sampson who in town would have an inventory extensive enough to hold certificates that would match that list. He said any bank. He mentioned three city brokers; one of them was Carter and Townsend."

Fenner gave the other names. "Both firms are larger than you, aren't they? Do more business? . . . Well, if you can match the list so can they."

"The difference," Townsend said, unable to hide his contempt, "is that you know for sure I'm carrying a load on my back that gets heavier most weeks. So maybe I could switch stock certificates and get my markers back, is that it?"

By then Laura was on her feet. There were unfriendly, challenging glints in the dark eyes, blotches of color on the cheekbones.

"You conned me, didn't you? Admit it. Into asking you up here for a fishing expedition."

Fenner had no answer for that but he could feel the growing warmth in his cheeks. Not wanting a confrontation, he was now faced with one. For a moment he decided he had played his hand badly but suddenly there popped from some crevice in his brain a contrary thought. If Bruce, characteristically not a suspicious or devious man, had no involvement would he take offense or sense any implication?

Fenner did not think so and there came to mind a line from somewhere about protesting too much. Shakespeare? He had it then—*The lady doth protest too much methinks.* All that had to be changed was the sex. Now, having no intention of disclosing that he had a witness as to Townsend's whereabouts Saturday morning, he stood up.

"That's your inference, Bruce. Obviously Ludlow brought stocks to town or there would have been no such list. There were no stocks around when I found him Monday morning. The official inference is that he was murdered for those stocks. Sorry if I loused up your dinner plans."

He started to put the photocopy back into his pocket. "I thought as a customer I could ask you"—and he also thought, *what a liar you are, Fenner*—"but I'll try your brother."

Townsend had come to his feet while Fenner spoke. Now he was face to face, taller, broader, handsomer, angrier. He was also a gentleman and able to contain that anger.

"Let's have it. What the hell—" He snatched the folded sheet. "If I don't check it someone else will. Just do me a favor, Jack. Stay away from Laura, okay?"

That seemed to say it all. Fenner shrugged and glanced at the woman but she was watching Townsend, her face thoughtful and concerned. He put down any thought of offering polite thanks for the drinks, turned without a word, and headed for the door.

15

ONCE AGAIN forced to dine alone, Jack Fenner picked a small Italian restaurant seldom frequented by friends or acquaintances. He ate his spaghetti with mushroom sauce and a green salad and drank a small carafe of Chianti in brooding silence, his mind a discouraging jumble of mixed thoughts not one of which was wholly acceptable. He topped off his meal with a slice of spumoni and coffee, managed a pleasant good night to the host, and went out to his car.

The night air seemed cooler on his five-block walk from the garage and he realized it was beginning to be topcoat weather. Recalling what had happened the night before, as he reached his block he was careful to inspect his front windows. There was no light now and he could tell the draperies had not been drawn. He had to push hard at the sticky downstairs door and he climbed absently, head down, conscious of the quiet in the old house and liking it.

He had the key in the door when he heard the whisper of sound somewhere close and he spun quickly, nerve-ends already tight and tingling. Even before his eyes could focus, instinct told him someone had been waiting on the stairs leading to the third-floor apartment, waiting out of sight on the dimly lighted landing for his arrival, and he thought, *Jesus! Does Matlock still think I've got that stock?*

Then he saw it, a moving shadow darker than the rest, all

black, it seemed, except for a white oval face beneath curly blond hair. Reflected light glinted from a gun barrel.

It was the blond wig that fooled him. Without it the woman became Ludlow's companion, Hildy Dryden, and the voice was familiar when she said, "Mr. Fenner, I've been waiting quite a while."

Fenner let his pent-up breath expel and felt his muscles relax. He finished unlocking the door, pocketed the keys. Still too surprised to let the gun bother him greatly he sighed again and said, "I guess you want to come in."

"Yes, please. And be nice, will you? Like you were at the motel."

Once past the tiny vestibule a light switch activated one floor lamp and one table lamp. He moved well inside before he turned to face her, watching her close the door behind her and aware of the quick, darting glance that flicked so carefully about the room he could not tell whether she was searching for spooks or mentally redecorating the place.

Satisfied, she asked him why he didn't sit down and he nodded and moved to the divan. There was a straight-back chair about ten feet away and she sat cautiously on the edge of it, handbag in her lap and the gun in her right hand.

"The wig fooled me," he said dryly.

That earned him a small smile. "Pretty horrible, isn't it? I knew the police would be looking for me. I found it in a secondhand boutique."

"With that on, you look like a hooker."

"I do?"

She sounded surprised, considered a moment; then reached up to remove it. When she shook out her own dark, short hair he nodded his approval and said she looked a lot better. As before, he had no intention of doing anything about the gun. He somehow doubted if she would use it, but with amateurs, particularly jittery ones, there was always some risk.

But there was, he admitted, a startling transformation between the girl he had seen at the motel and this one. With almost no makeup, her face had a fresh young look, but perhaps it was the dress that made the most difference. It was the black one he had seen her fold and put in the suitcase before adding the envelope.

Simply cut, with a rounded neck, knee length, she had now an almost demure appearance with none of the original brashness showing. In addition she seemed not only confident but completely at ease.

"How'd you know where to find me?"

"I saw your wallet, remember?"

"I thought you'd be long gone," he said, still trying to find some reason for her presence and getting nowhere. "Have you still got that envelope? You know, the one I saw you pack?"

She bobbed her head, completely unperturbed.

"And you know what's in it, right?" She nodded again. "The stock certificates Ludlow brought from New York." When silence greeted the remark he said, "Can I ask a question? Just what the hell are you hanging around for?"

She took a moment to reply and he watched her mouth tighten, some stubbornness working on her chin.

"Because," she said finally and with a noticeable defiance in her tone, "I want to get what I came for."

"And what's that?"

"The twenty-five hundred I was going to steal from Les."

Fenner knew he was squinting; he couldn't help it.

"Did you say steal?"

"It was the only way I could get it. Les was to get five thousand for doing the job and I'd been waiting for a chance to split, and I didn't want to go back home unless I had enough to live on a while. Anyway he'd sponged and borrowed almost that much while we were together. . . . What I was going to do," she said, still defiant, "was spike his drinks that night, grab my share of the five, and run. Only I never got the chance, did I? Some bastard shot him."

"Yeah," said Fenner with undisguised skepticism. "And if you didn't know he was dead how'd you get that envelope?"

"All I know is it was there. I think he put the envelope on that settee in your office when he came in and then tossed his raincoat on top of it. The only reason I saw it is because when I'd emptied his pockets I thought I'd better take the coat too."

"All right." Fenner shook his head. He took a slow, deliberate breath, let it escape between pursed lips, fighting disbelief as he told himself to be patient. "Is it all right to ask just what you want from me?"

"I have to talk to someone. I don't know anybody else, and I can't go back to the New York place, and you were pretty decent out at the motel and—oh, I don't know," she wailed, no longer so sure of herself. "I guess it was just another of my bum ideas." She seemed at the point of tears and started to rise. Fenner stopped her.

"Hold it. Relax."

For a moment the dark eyes watched him narrowly, her indecision fading as her confidence grew. When Fenner sensed her relief he felt a smile coming; he also realized he was beginning to like this spunky girl with the pretty face and snub nose, a bewildered waif wanting comforting.

"You took a chance coming here, even with that wig. You waited a long time. You want to talk and, as you say, I'm a pretty decent guy. I also listen good. Suppose you start by telling me your name. It isn't Ludlow according to the New York cops."

"Dryden. Hildy Dryden."

He nodded, pleased that this corresponded with the name Bacon had received from the New York City authorities.

"From where? Originally?"

"Ohio. Sandusky. Ever hear of it?"

"Sure. West of Cleveland."

"On the lake."

"So what brought you to New York. Run away from home?"

"Sort of."

"With a guy?"

He watched the change come, the slackening of tension, a new softness in the eyes as she watched him.

"A drummer," she said with a tiny grimace. "And you know something? Drummers are the nuttiest guys in a band—except maybe some trombone players."

"A local character?"

"Oh, no. Across the bay from Sandusky is what used to be an amusement park. It's nicer now, higher class. Well, we used to go over there Saturday nights in the summer. Sometimes double-dating, sometimes two or three of us girls, you know, sort of wanting for something nice to happen, willing to be picked up if the guys looked right and didn't expect you to put out just because they bought you a drink. That's how I met Charlie, only it was a Sunday afternoon and the band was off. He bought me dinner and we talked and had some laughs and he didn't proposition me; not then."

A small smile had begun to work at the corners of her mouth, as though the remembrance of such times made the nostalgia pleasurable.

"He was fun to be with," she said wistfully. "Always a lot of laughs, and he was never mean until later; by Labor Day I was sort of in love with him, I guess. Anyway that's what I told myself. And the band was going to work itself east in a few days and he said why didn't I come with him. . . . Well, things had been pretty rough at home for a long time. My stepfather was always after me and I was afraid I'd get raped or beat up, and my mother was more interested in the bottle than me.

"I was clerking in a drugstore after I got out of high school, but I had to pay board at home and I hadn't saved much, and I'd always wanted to go to New York." She paused, giving other memories a chance to surface.

"There was a hometown boy I'd been going with some, sort of a boy-next-door type. Nice and not bad-looking but dull, you know? Too much of a square, is what I thought then. He was a senior in college, studying pharmacy because his uncle owned the drugstore I worked in. But I don't know, I was kind of sick of the drugstore bit, and the New York idea sounded more exciting I guess."

She sighed, seemed to notice the gun, and shifted it to her left hand.

"Do you need that thing?" Fenner said, pointing.

"I hope not," she said when she had considered the question. "But you're still a private cop. If I didn't have it you might feel you had to take me in. I think I could hit a leg or something if you started to crowd me and I thought you meant it."

It was a point well taken and Fenner was willing to concede it. Ethically he was obligated to notify Lieutenant Bacon, but the gun was excuse enough to postpone any such decision.

"You've got a point, Hildy," he said, and reached for cigarettes. "So you ran off with Charlie. What made you split?"

"Because he kept trying to turn me on with cocaine, that's why." After a sober moment the smile started again and she said, "It was a fun trip mostly. There were four or five wives traveling on the band's bus and they, you know, sort of accepted me because everybody liked Charlie. I'd smoke a joint with him most times, who doesn't? I knew he was sniffing too. It sort of bugged me, and when he started trying to force me to get with it I got kind of scared. I knew by then I was going to split once we hit New York and the time he really belted me around because I wouldn't turn on was when we were in Albany. So I just took off for a bus ride of my own."

Fenner, wanting to get to the Ludlow part of her story but willing to wait and preferring it to be voluntary, said, "Look, Hildy, we've still got some talking to do, you know? About Ludlow and that envelope, and why you've been hanging around since Saturday morning. So how about a drink?"

"Well—I guess not."

"You don't mind if I do?"

"Where is it?" A touch of uncertainty returning.

"In the kitchen."

"Okay. I'll go with you if you promise to behave."

Fenner's grin was genuine and his angular face was at ease.

"Like I have been."

This time her smile was broad and genuine, adding to her pixy attractiveness.

"Just like that."

She had a little trouble as she stood up. At first she tucked the wig under one arm, which left one hand for the gun and one for the handbag. Not liking the arrangement, she backed a few steps to get more room, put the gun carefully on an end table, and took time to cram the wig into her bag. When she was ready she motioned Fenner toward the inner hall.

"You don't mind if I tag along, you know, just in case?"

Fenner said he wouldn't have it any other way and he could hear her behind him as he went into the kitchen, got an ice tray out, and wrenched some cubes onto the counter. He took a bottle from the cabinet above, put three cubes in an old-fashioned glass, poured to within an inch of the top, added water. As he turned she said:

"What's that you're drinking?"

"Bourbon."

"Would you have any Scotch? I mean if I changed my mind?"

He reached again, producing a bottle of White Label. "Long or short?"

She was leaning against the doorframe now, her expression amused. "Just like yours, please."

When he finished she backed in front of him, giving him room, the gun muzzle angling downward but her grip firm. Once again in the living room she indicated he was to put her glass beside the same chair she had been using, then waited for Fenner to resume his seat.

"So how and where did you meet Leslie Ludlow, Hildy?"

"Where I was doing the topless, go-go bit. It was a joint, but better than some of the traps I'd been in. The pay was real good but, man, it was hard work. Leslie had already been coming in before I started and he seemed a lot nicer than most of the creeps who wanted to take me home. He was older and dressed neater and he didn't crowd and he was a good spender. Also he was from Ohio, too. Cincinnati. Oh, I knew he wasn't any bank president and later I found he did things for the mob. I had an idea he was on the hustle even at first but so what? He was always pretty decent and, oh, I don't know, maybe I was just tired of making it alone, tired of the long-hair types; I know now I was just kidding myself. I guess I was even thinking of marriage when I finally moved in with him.

"It was okay for a while. He was away a lot; two or three days at a time. And he wasn't making all that much. First thing I knew I was paying the rent—I'd saved quite a lot from the go-go thing—and buying the groceries and lending him twenty or fifty and not getting any of it back."

"He wouldn't buy the marriage idea?"

"No way." She shook her head, a momentary gesture of defeat. "He told me why. He'd been married and his wife shot him and would have killed the girl he was with if she'd been a better shot. He kept a newspaper clipping in his wallet to prove it. It told how he was recovering and how bail was reduced for his wife. He said he hadn't seen her since, that she stuck the bail bondsman, cleaned out the apartment, and took off before he got out of the hospital. He'd been unlucky once, he said, and he wasn't about to take another chance.

"But what really changed my mind was something that happened back home," she said, some new softness in her voice. "You know this boy I told you about? Well, he got married after he graduated. His wife had a baby, and a year or so later she was driving along when some crazy kids in a stolen car ran a stop sign. Killed her but not the baby. The thing I read said one kid got a cut lip and the other was uninjured.

"The reason I read it at all is because I used to buy the Sandusky paper when I thought of it from an out-of-town-paper newsstand. So when I knew what happened I bought a sympathy card and wrote a little note. About two weeks later I got an answer."

Again the silence came and now there was a definite mistiness in the dark eyes that seemed unaware of Fenner or anything else in the room.

"It was sweet," she said, her voice hardly more than a whisper. "And I answered it and—well we started to correspond. You know, not love letters, just two friends. And that's when I began to think I had a way out that could be worthwhile and permanent. I knew somehow that Howard still liked me a lot and he said he was a partner in the drugstore now, and I finally woke up and realized I could have had it all if I hadn't been such a silly little bitch. Howard's mother is taking care of the child now, and maybe, who knows, he might like another wife. Me.

"I had to have some money," she said, her gaze steady now as she focused on Fenner. "Leslie had just about tapped me out. But I'd never live at home again. I had to have enough to get a place of my own and carry me decently until I found the right thing to do and gave Howard a chance. So when Les came in last Friday morning with this brown envelope you'd have thought he struck oil. He said did I know what was in it? Four hundred thousand. And I asked him was it counterfeit, and he said it was worth that to the right guy and he was to deliver it and bring something back and he was to get paid five thousand for the job.

"I knew I was going to come up here with him," she said decisively. "I already told you how I'd figured to lift half of it and take off for Sandusky. I wasn't even going back to the apartment. What few clothes I had could stay there."

"All right." Fenner swallowed half his drink, believing what he had heard. "So you were at the Starlight Friday night and you drove downtown with him Saturday morning in the rental car."

"Sure. Because I didn't know just when he'd collect his five and I intended to stick right with him until I got a chance to get my half. You know, in case he should decide to ditch me."

"You sat waiting in the car. He told you where he was coming, but not who he was going to meet."

"Right. We weren't parked facing the entrance but that didn't bother me because I knew he had to come back to the car. I don't know how long it was. Maybe three-quarters of an hour, and I was getting more uptight every minute. When I couldn't stand it any longer I went up to your office and there he was on the floor in front of the coffee table."

"So you emptied his pockets."

"Yes, and don't ask me why. I guess I'd sort of flipped seeing him like that. I didn't have any ideas, I just did it."

"Did you find any markers?"

"What markers?"

Fenner let it go. "But you discovered the envelope under the raincoat."

"I told you I did."

"So why did you take a cab? Why didn't you use your car?"

"I don't know that either. I was in a fog and panicky and scared to death. I didn't even think about the car, or if I did I probably had some crazy idea someone might be watching it."

"But you came back and got it later."

"Sunday afternoon. There were only a couple other cars on the street and hardly anybody around. But I watched a long time from the corner before I got up nerve enough to try it."

"Okay, Hildy. Now give me one good reason why you risked staying in town all this time."

"I told you."

"Tell me again."

She stuck her chin out at him, jaw muscles tightening. "I want what I came for—my half. Twenty-five hundred."

Fenner finished his drink, considered a refill, rejected the idea. He felt a grudging admiration for the girl's spunk and determination but he also felt obligated to explain the risk she was running.

"You didn't come here just to talk, did you?"

"I didn't?" Her surprise seemed genuine.

"You must have wanted advice. So I'll give you some. You know what's in that envelope, don't you?"

"I do now."

"You also know Ludlow had mob connections, that this is a mob job. Right now they've got guys out on the streets just like the police. Looking for you and that envelope."

He went on to explain how his apartment had been searched and his office file cabinet jimmied.

"A man named Matlock is doing the looking. He knows why Ludlow came and what he carried. He knows I found the body and maybe he still isn't sure I didn't lift that envelope. He sure as hell knows about you, and the New York people have to be watching your apartment."

He leaned forward, his voice flat, direct, and intent. "If you go to the police while you can, I mean right now, and turn over the envelope and tell your story they may hold you in detention while they check it out, but you'll still be alive when you walk out, assuming you're telling the truth."

"Well, I am."

"But if Matlock's people find you with that envelope, the odds are nine to five you'll never get to Sandusky to marry Howard and have any babies. You have a room somewhere, right? Is the envelope in that room?" He watched her nod. "Then get rid of it."

"I can't just throw it away," she said, the thought shocking her.

"Then do this while you make up your mind. Take it down to South Station, pick a locker on the main concourse, take the key. And remember your quarter is only good for twenty-four hours so you'll have to put in a quarter a day if you don't want it opened by some attendant."

For the next five seconds she sat as still as a statue, her eyes widening as she considered the suggestion. Very slowly then she reached down for her glass and gulped the rest of her drink. She put the glass back, reaching for the handbag without shifting her gaze. Still groping blindly, she removed the wig. Placing the gun within easy reach, she donned the wig and patted it in place. When she was ready she stood up and said:

"I suppose you have to tell the police. And they'll start looking for a blonde. So—" She let the word hang, and tipped her small head an inch. When Fenner saw the curl at the corner of her mouth and what could only be a mischievous light in her eyes, he could only gape at such unexpected poise and resiliency. "I guess," she said as she started to back away, "I'll have to find one with red hair, or maybe platinum."

Fenner tried once more to make her understand the risk she was running.

"You think I've been trying to snow you?"

"About what?"

"You're bucking some real mean boys. You could wind up dead."

"I know. Only I've got myself a plan."

"Great. Go ahead, press your luck."

"What luck?"

"You're walking around, aren't you?" Fenner saw he was wasting his breath and let it go with a quip. "And where else are you going to find a lovable character like me for a friend?"

This time her laugh was quick and merry. "That's what I mean. Just knowing a sweet man like you makes me know I'll stay lucky."

She was in the entryway then, and out of sight, and Fenner, still battling his disbelief, sat where he was until he heard the door close. Only then did he realize that he really did need another drink.

16

WEDNESDAY WAS another nice morning. While Fenner stood at a kitchen counter sipping coffee, with the radio on, the local weatherman said that the weather would be in the high seventies, with a probability of afternoon showers. Because he thought some exercise might sweep the cobwebs from his mind and activate his brain sufficiently to work intelligently, lucidly, and to some purpose, he walked all the way to his office.

Alice was again working on her needlepoint, one knee crossed and the blond hair falling down both sides of her face. The mail had not yet been delivered but his inner office looked as if it had just been dusted, everything neat and the green carafe filled with ice water, the two clean glasses standing on the matching tray.

For perhaps five minutes Fenner leaned back in his chair, his green gaze angling upward, unfocused and full of indecision. Then, with the connecting door open, he called out to ask Alice to dial police headquarters. When he had a reply he named an extension and presently Bacon answered, his familiar voice gruff and businesslike. By that time Fenner had decided to come directly to the point and forget the amenities.

"Have you found Ludlow's girlfriend?"

"No."

"Well, you'd better put out a new description to the precincts. She's a blonde now, or was last night."

The statement brought a noticeable silence followed by a now familiar growl.

"How the hell do you know?"

Fenner recited a carefully prepared account. He had given some thought as to how much he could say and how he would say it. Now he spoke in quick, unaccented tones, each sentence right on top of the preceding one so Bacon would have no chance to interrupt or question the account. He did not mention the envelope or the suggestion he had made to Hildy Dryden. When he finished, Bacon at once asked a question Fenner was unprepared to answer.

"What the hell is it with you, Jack? Every cop in town looking for that broad and she comes to you. With a gun again, right? And you have to let her walk out. So give me one good reason why she came at all. What did she expect from you anyway?"

What indeed? Fenner thought. He could make no positive or definitive answer because he was not sure he had one. All he could do was try and see how Bacon reacted to the only half-reasonable reply he could think of.

"She never did say, Lieutenant. All I can give you is the impression I got."

"Which was?"

"She was frightened, mixed up, lost. She was out of her depth and she knew it. I didn't try to pressure her out at the motel Monday morning. She realized Ludlow had mob connections and she was scared; but for some reason not of me. All I could do was give her a piece of advice."

"Which was?"

"Turn herself in."

"Well, that's something." Bacon's tone was sardonic. "Thanks a lot."

"I told her it might be the best way to stay alive, that there'd be mob guys on the street looking for her, just like you're doing."

"Yeah. Okay. If she shows again, grab her, hunh? You've

handled tougher assignments than that, gun or no gun. Where's your pride?" Then, as an afterthought: "Why couldn't I have some of that personal magnetism you've got? Father confessor to strange young chicks . . . We'll get her, you know. And her story better check with yours, Jack. Okay?"

The connection broke before Fenner could respond and he was still considering the lieutenant's warning when Alice buzzed him. When he said, "Yes," she said, "There's a Miss Latimer to see you."

He was around the desk and at the door to greet her when she came in, and he was at once aware of the severity of her manner. The smooth olive face was wooden, the dark eyes had worried lights, and her black hair was again pulled back in workaday fashion. A plain gray woolen dress had been substituted for the business suit he had seen before and she carried a lightweight coat over one arm.

Because Fenner could not even guess what brought her he did not try but said, "Good morning," and indicated a chair in front of the desk as he closed the door. She made no reply but seated herself, studying him a moment before she spoke.

"That friendly, phony visit of yours last night really blew our evening."

"Oh?"

"Because we had a fight after you left. Not a fight, really. We just had it out about this gambling debt he owes and what has been happening to him. I knew he was in trouble because I'd get a call sometimes. A man with a menacing voice demanding he call some number; then phoning the next day and wanting to know why Bruce hadn't called, warning if he didn't I should reserve a hospital bed."

She made a shrugging gesture with one hand and shoulder, her dark gaze still intent, nothing changing in her voice.

"Bruce would never tell me why or how much he owed. He'd made a silly bet once and he was paying off; he could handle it. I finally nagged the details out of him."

"Then you know what the total is?"

"Yes. But I'm not going to tell you. I also made him admit that the pressure was getting worse. If you know Bruce you know he's sometimes more reckless than smart and I don't think this is the time for him to do something foolish."

"He could be in an even tougher financial bind," Fenner said.

"Oh, how could he?"

"I think a judge might rule that he had abandoned his wife. She could demand and probably get support payments."

"She's got enough."

"So you said yesterday afternoon. That doesn't prevent wives from trying to punish and harass the husband out of sheer perversity. Bruce just happened to be lucky in that respect."

The remark did not seem either to bother or concern her and he knew that behind the pretty dark face and the lithe and sexually oriented body this was a self-sufficient, determined woman who intended to survive.

"Frankly I'm worried," she said, as though there had been no digression. She leaned forward, her phrases clipped and businesslike. "Could you arrange for a man to stay near him for a few days, keep an eye on him? Someone experienced enough to protect him if necessary?"

Fenner had his answer then. He could understand such concern but he had to be honest about the problem she faced.

"You mean someone like a bodyguard?"

"I guess so."

"I could, yes. I know a half-dozen competent men who work for a reasonable hourly charge." It was his turn to lean forward, forearms on the desk. "But would Bruce agree to such an arrangement?"

That made her think and her frown accented her uncertainty. "Why would he have to know? I thought we could arrange this between us."

Fenner shook his head and said, "I'm afraid not. Any

bodyguard would have to remain fairly close to be of any use in a pinch. Bruce would have to notice him before too long, and he's just the type that would go up to your man and ask him what the hell he was doing."

"And there isn't any other way?"

"Not and be effective. You'd be wasting your money, Miss Latimer."

She said, "Oh," and he could see the thrust of her breasts against the fabric of her dress. After a moment she looked down at her folded hands. Defeat showed in the growing slackness in her face but before she could make any comment, Alice buzzed him again. The buzzer was still going when the door opened suddenly and Maurie Matlock strode in followed by a tall broad blond man of thirty or so.

Aware now of the woman, Matlock stopped short. His initiative lost, he seemed both baffled and annoyed as he glanced from one to the other before he tried to cover his rudeness.

"Sorry," he said grudgingly. "I didn't know you were busy."

"You could have asked my secretary, Maurie," Fenner said coldly. "That's what she's there for."

"Yeah—well—"

Laura Latimer broke the impasse by coming to her feet. She smoothed out her dress and picked up her coat. The look she gave Matlock was both hateful and contemptuous.

"I was just leaving," she said, and nodded to Fenner. "I'll think about what you said."

Fenner walked her to the door but she ignored him as she strode through the anteroom. Alice, open-eyed and flushed, offered a shrug of helplessness. Fenner winked at her, closed his office door, went behind his desk, and took time to study Matlock and his younger companion, a good-looking empty-faced fellow who had the height, weight, and muscular configuration of a tight end.

Matlock, sitting down now, was shorter, blockier, plumper.

His face was broad, a growing puffiness accenting the small, bright, observant little eyes. Only the sides and back of his head had hair; the bald top looked pink and healthy.

About fifty or more now, he had once, when very young, been an odd-job enforcer for Shylocks until he had earned the right to set up a moneylending district of his own. Never an actual Mafia member, he had set up a workable arrangement with the Providence don, at the same time maintaining some reciprocal understanding with the New York people. Now many years later he was the head man at Matlock Enterprises with investments, some hidden according to the word on the street, in apartments, laundries, a construction outfit specializing in suburban condominiums, all apparently profitable. Bookmaking as a business he left to others these days, except in cases like Townsend's where the wager was sizeable and the odds and potential profits were too tempting to be ignored.

His eyes were busy as he lit a cigar and flipped the match in the general direction of the desk. He looked casually about, his glance lingering longest on the still unrepaired filing cabinet. Fenner waited, not liking the man, not knowing what had brought him here, and not giving a damn. He looked at the big blond long enough and disdainfully enough to bring a flush to the cheeks, but he kept his own mounting resentment under control.

When he was ready Matlock crossed his knees and said, "You got this place wired?"

"No."

"But you got a tape machine."

"Certainly. I use it sometimes in interviews with clients so the record will be straight in case of any misunderstanding later on. But they know I'm using it."

"Show me."

Fenner opened the bottom drawer and brought forth a compact but expensive recorder. He put it in the middle of the desk.

At a word from Matlock the blond picked it up to make sure

there was no outside connection or wire. Satisfied, Matlock said:

"I'll make it quick, Fenner. We've been looking for an envelope; we still are."

"I know," Fenner said with open disdain. "It contained four hundred grand in hot stock that was brought up here by a two-bit runner who got himself killed in my office. Because I found him I might have lifted that envelope. You tried my apartment, and here and—"

"We're gonna keep on looking. We stopped by to drop a thought on you. There could be places where that envelope could be. You could know about it. In case you do, and we find it out, it's going to cost you."

"I know," Fenner said, very quiet now but still nasty. "And then I'll have an accident."

"I thought you'd get the idea. Because this is not really my bag. It's a New York operation basically; I'm just overseeing this end. And when you cross those guys down there they don't always listen to reason."

"The stocks were hot," Fenner said. "Part of a bigger hit. And maybe they were brought up here to exchange for some certificates not so hot."

"That's your guess?"

"Based on some digging," Fenner said, and again repeated his discussion with Fred Sampson at the *Courier*. "But if you want your envelope you better start thinking about Ludlow's cute girlfriend."

"We are. We are."

He started to push back his chair and Fenner said, "Got another minute? I've been kicking around a half-baked theory. Thought you might like to hear it."

"Why not?"

Fenner looked at the big blond. "What's your name?"

"Fred," said the man through thin lips.

"You want Freddie to hear this?"

Matlock turned and inspected his companion. For the first

time he allowed himself a smile, as a doting father might at a favorite son.

"Freddie's my man Friday. What's the theory?"

"Bruce Townsend went for thirty quite a while ago. Some weeks he gets up the vigorish, sometimes no. He signs more markers. His old man won't help him out; he's probably borrowed all he can. If he was pressed enough and began to worry about his health, if you convinced him you couldn't wait for his old man to die so he could inherit the trust money, he might be ripe for a proposition that would get him off the hook for good."

"Such as?"

"Exchanging good clean cold stock certificates from the firm's inventory for some of the hot ones grabbed in that New York heist a few weeks back."

He went on to describe the list he had taken from Ludlow's coat pocket and said, "The complete rundown of all certificates taken in New York could have been mailed up to you; Townsend could check his inventory in advance and find out how many he could match.

"New York," he added, "sends Ludlow up with the proper certificates, proper number of shares. Townsend meets him in my office, makes the exchange in return for his markers, knowing he can put the hot shares back in the vault Monday morning and hoping they will be undiscovered for a long time. A chunk of nice clean cold stock for the New York boys, an adequate cut for you, but more than enough to cancel Townsend's debt so he can get his markers back and breathe again."

When Fenner finished Matlock studied him a moment, the deepset eyes blank, detached. He nodded once. "I like it," he said. "I should have thought of something like that before."

"Yeah." Fenner's sleepy gaze was unwavering. "The trouble is, it's only a theory now. Someone knocked off your boy Ludlow either before or after the switch was made. Either way a very valuable envelope is missing or you wouldn't be trying to locate it. You may still have the markers but the New York crowd must be getting a little sore by now, a thing like that happening in your territory."

Matlock stood up, nothing changing in his blocky face. The question he asked seemed wholly unrelated to what had been said.

"That chick I walked in on. Townsend's, right?"

Fenner nodded, wondering what came next.

"You think she knows about the markers?"

"I do now. I think she nagged the truth out of Townsend last night. . . . How much does it come to, Maurie? The total to date. How much has he already paid?"

If Matlock heard the question he ignored it. "What did she want from you, Fenner?"

Fenner just looked at him, his grin mean and disdainful. When Matlock understood that there was to be no reply, he turned and left the room, Freddie at his heels.

17

WHEN MATLOCK LEFT, Alice Maxwell came in and put the morning mail in front of him, the envelopes properly slit for his inspection. During the next half-hour he endorsed two sizeable checks which Alice would deposit during her lunch break. He wrote and signed three others for her to mail to firms he owed. He dictated replies to two inquiries, and when she withdrew and closed the door he leaned back, cradling his neck with laced fingers.

He was not sure how long he stayed that way, his lean face somber, his gaze fixed and sightless as he tried to review everything he had learned during the past three days in an effort to find a hypothesis that was in some measure acceptable. He did not hope to arrive at any definitive conclusion but he continued to inspect and consider all possibilities until he discovered a line of reasoning heretofore too deeply embedded in the back of his brain even to warrant inspection. In the hope of giving this new idea more substance, he swiveled, examined the bookcase behind the desk, and selected a small black-bound volume.

This was a national directory of supposedly reputable detective agencies deemed worthy of listing. A few he recognized as well-known outfits with branches in most of the states including Puerto Rico. Most, however, meant nothing to him, the common names like Acme and Apex duplicated over and over since there seemed to be only so many terms suitable to the profession. The listings were arranged both alphabetically and geographically and he turned to Ohio and Cincinnati. He could not find a single contact in the area but he did recognize one organization that had a local branch and now, hope rising, he saw how he might handle the problem.

For he knew two men who worked out of this office; he had in fact been offered a job there before deciding to try it on his own. Such a discovery gave birth to a small spark of enthusiasm and when he found a number he dialed and asked for Ed O'Neil.

"Ed," he said when O'Neil came on. "Jack Fenner."

"Well, well. How goes it with you, Jack?"

The voice sounded both surprised and friendly and when the pleasantries had been exchanged Fenner made his request.

"Do you, or does anyone in your office, know anyone in your Cincinnati branch? Would you ask around?"

"I don't have to, Jack. Guy named Sam Wilson. He was transferred from this office about a year ago; grew up around there."

"Great!" said Fenner, feeling another small lift to his spirits. "Can I have the phone number of your office there?"

O'Neil said to hold on and seconds later he gave Fenner the area code and city number.

Deciding to make the call person-to-person after he had hung up, Fenner asked Alice to try it. "I want to speak to Sam Wilson. If he's not there see if you can find out how long he'll be gone."

He had his answer within seconds. Mr. Wilson had stepped out of the office but was expected back in fifteen or twenty minutes. Word had been left to return the call.

When Alice had done her part she asked if she should wait or could she go to lunch now. Fenner told her to go ahead and was at the same time astonished to discover it was already twelve-thirty. While he waited in the quiet of the office he found a note pad and began to jot down the information he wanted, the questions that should be asked. He was still thinking of the proper approach when the call came.

When he heard Sam Wilson's voice he identified himself and explained how Ed O'Neil had given him Wilson's name. Once he understood the situation Wilson became both friendly and cooperative as Fenner stated his requests.

"You can check with your boss," he said. "If he doesn't want you to handle it ask him to put someone else on it. It shouldn't take long or too much legwork. You could probably do most of it by phone if you've got contacts at police headquarters and in the city or county department of vital statistics or whatever they call it out there.

"The guy I'm interested in is named Ludlow. Leslie Ludlow. At least that's the name he's been using in New York. He should have a minor rap sheet in Cincinnati. Worked for some credit bureau until he got bounced. I know he's in the police files because his wife put him in the hospital with a slug in his shoulder. I don't remember how long ago. Apparently a few years."

He explained the background as he knew it; then asked the questions, reading from his note pad. When he finished, Wilson said it shouldn't be any problem.

"I can probably check most of it out right here at my desk."

"Beautiful," Fenner said happily. "Call back when you have it. This afternoon if possible and the earlier the better." He gave his area code and number. "If I'm out my secretary will take down what you have. And thanks a million, Sam. Stick your bill in the mail and I'll get a check back to your office."

Somehow the thought that he would now have help in exploring this tenuous line of reasoning was encouraging and he let his imagination take flight until he realized he was hungry. The idea of another sandwich from across the street held no appeal, so he locked his door and left a note for Alice on her desk.

Once on the street he turned right toward the center of the city, having no destination and unable as yet to make a decision. Overhead cloud patches gave a bit of substance to the weather prediction of probable showers but the breeze had not yet shifted into the east. Unaware of others who shared the sidewalks unless it was necessary to dodge an impending collision, he turned right on Berkeley and passed police headquarters without stopping. He had turned left on Stuart when a new thought suggested itself and he continued on to Jake Wirth's, a restaurant he had not visited in months. Once inside, he saw the interior was, as always, the same old wooden floors, the sawdust, the long busy bar, the elderly waiters.

The luncheon rush was nearly over and he took a table as far away from those that were occupied as possible. He noticed two or three acquaintances who waved and he responded. There was a large table at which several student types were discussing with spirit the coming inevitable disintegration of the country and the utter chaos that must follow.

Closing his ears to such nonsense, he considered ordering a house specialty—frankfurts; not the long, thin, wizened variety so often served by quick-food chains, but fat and juicy and pink. But when the waiter stopped beside him he fell back on an old standard, a hot roast-beef sandwich and a stein of light beer.

He took his time when the order came, oblivious to the noisy surroundings and alone with his thoughts. He considered a second beer when he finished the sandwich but made the first one last while he smoked two cigarettes. When he paid the check and left a generous tip he was surprised to see that it was after two, and this moved him to rise and head for the pay telephone, where he dialed his office. Not expecting anything from Cincinnati yet, he nevertheless asked.

"Not yet, Mr. Fenner," Alice said. "But there is something you might want to do something about."

"What?"

"A letter, I guess; an envelope anyway. Hand addressed to you and delivered by messenger."

"When?"

"Not five minutes ago. It's got something in it. I mean more than just paper."

"Like a bomb maybe?"

The remark brought the expected quick small sound of laughter.

"No. Unless it's small and sort of flat."

Fenner thanked her and said he would be back in five minutes if he could snag a cruising cab. . . .

Alice Maxwell handed Fenner the envelope as soon as he closed the outer door, a look of anticipation dancing in her eyes. He saw at once that it was a plain, letter-size envelope of the chainstore variety. His name had been written in a round girlish hand and he could tell at once that it contained something other than a sheet of paper.

"Who brought it, Alice? You said a messenger. In a uniform of some kind?"

"Just a man. Young, shaggy-haired, ordinary-looking. I thought maybe a taxi driver. When I started to tip him he shook his head and said the lady had given him ten dollars to deliver it."

Fenner nodded absently and turned away, seeing the girl's look of disappointment as Alice realized he intended to inspect the contents in private. With his door closed, Fenner carefully slit the envelope and as he removed the note a key slid into his fingers.

He turned it over twice, noting the number stamped on the round end and making a quick guess as to where it had come from. Then he was reading the note written in the same rounded handwriting on paper from which the top had been cut, suggesting that it might well have been a piece of hotel stationery. The single paragraph without salutation read:

I got what I came for and I took your advice. Because you're the only man I've met in the last couple of years I felt I could trust I'm making

*you a present of the enclosed. Do what you think best with it. I hope
you won't have to tell my real name because I'm on my way to you
know where. If Howard and I get together I'll send you a Christmas
card.*

There was no signature. None was needed. If Hildy Dryden
had followed his advice to the letter, somewhere in the long
main concourse of South Station was a locker containing four
hundred thousand dollars in stock certificates. Possibly legitimate; more likely stolen.

For minutes he sat where he was, eyes on the note, his busy
mind grooving his brow above half-open lids. Slowly then he
refolded the sheet and slid it far back in a lower drawer of
his desk. The key he tucked beneath the handkerchief in his
right-hand hip pocket. Then he leaned back and began his
wait, trying to be patient, trying even harder to keep his mind
a blank.

The way it turned out, Sam Wilson had done his job in
Cincinnati efficiently, thoroughly, and more quickly than
Fenner had believed possible. It was 3:42 when the call came
through and he heard the investigator's voice. When Fenner
asked if Wilson had had any luck, Wilson said there was
nothing to it since what Fenner wanted was all pretty much a
matter of record.

"You got a pencil and a piece of paper?" he asked. "So here
goes."

Sam Wilson delivered his information like the professional
he was, his words measured and distinct. For his part Fenner
was content to write down the facts, interrupting but once
when he said, "Covington . . . yeah." All this took perhaps
four minutes and then Wilson said, "That's it. Is it what you
wanted?"

"Exactly. And what you came up with is a hell of a lot more
than I hoped to get. I appreciate it, Sam, and remember—if
you ever need anything in my town, just say the word and it's
yours."

When he rang off there were excited glints deep down in Jack Fenner's green eyes and now, with some corroboration bolstering his confidence, he was nearly ready to accept a premise that had once been nothing more than a nebulous and unlikely possibility. With another glance at his watch he swiveled his chair and consulted an atlas he kept in the bookcase. After a minute or so he closed it and reached for the telephone directory. When he had jotted down a number, he pushed a button at the base of the instrument for an outside line, and dialed.

The voice that answered was female and sounded bored. "Matlock Enterprises. Good afternoon."

"Mr. Matlock, please. Mr. Fenner calling."

"One moment, please."

There was a sound of distant ringing and a second, brighter female voice said, "Mr. Matlock's office."

"Is this his secretary?"

"Yes, it is."

"This is Jack Fenner. I have to speak to Mr. Matlock. He knows me. You can say it's important."

Another pause and then a man's voice. "Fenner? This is Fred. Mr. Matlock's tied up. He isn't returning any calls."

"For how long?"

"He didn't say."

Fenner, his annoyance and mounting impatience difficult to curb, replied in curt, demanding tones.

"You better break in on him, Freddie. And get it straight the first time. You tell Maurie it has to do with the envelope he's been looking for and bugging me about. Tell him if he doesn't get on the horn now I'll know where to take it."

Apparently Freddie delivered the message because the next voice was Matlock's.

"What's this about that envelope, Fenner?"

"I'll tell you when I see you."

"When?"

"Now. If you've got a meeting or if you're romancing some

broad, break it up. I'll be in your building as soon as I can get a cab and if I don't get in I'll know what to do."

He hung up before Matlock could reply, satisfaction warping his lips. After a few seconds of such indulgence he regrouped his thoughts and dialed another number. This time the operator's voice seemed more cultivated as she said:

"Carter and Townsend."

"Mr. Bruce Townsend, please."

This time Townsend answered his own phone and Fenner spoke his piece, making his words deliberately ambiguous and faintly threatening as he stated that it was important for Townsend to meet him.

"At Laura's place," he finished, "if you're going to drive her home."

"I don't know," Townsend stalled, a note of doubt in the cadence of his voice. "I mean, I don't know if she wants to see you."

"Then convince her." Fenner paused, considered his phrasing, and spoke distinctly. "Look, Bruce. I know a lot more about those murders Saturday morning than I did when I saw you last night. There's no way I can avoid telling the police what I know and still keep my license. I just thought I ought to tell you first so you'll know what to expect. If you don't want it that way—"

"All right, all right," Townsend cut in irritably. "I'll get in touch with Laura. I don't know what you expect to prove, or if this is just another of your rude fishing expeditions, but we'll be there. We'll meet you outside. You can wait for us."

18

Haymarket Square was busy as always at that time of day. The clouds had taken charge in the late afternoon and the breeze, brisker now, carried a feeling of dampness in from the harbor. The sidewalks were filling from the early outpouring of nearby office buildings, and traffic crawled with exasperating slowness.

Fenner, on the edge of the seat, muttered savagely at each red light, and when the taxi stopped for another one a block from his destination he paid the driver and said he could make better time walking and the driver said so could a turtle. He was not, he tried to tell himself, in that much of a hurry. The few minutes saved by picking his way through the homeward-bound pedestrians were of no real importance. His impatience came from some inner source spawned by the conviction that he finally had a course of action that might prove productive.

Matlock Enterprises was on the seventh floor in one of the buildings close by the new complex of government structures in a renewal area once a bawdy, rundown neighborhood. As he stepped from the elevator, he saw the firm occupied a suite at the end of the hall to his right. The name had been lettered on one of the pebble-glass doors and he entered a reception room that had a clean, modern, antiseptic air.

A hall opened directly across from the entrance. A sizeable enclosure had been partitioned off by wood-and-glass walls, beyond which stood eight or ten desks, half of them occupied by office workers or clerks. The receptionist, a thirtyish woman with auburn hair, looked up from her magazine as Fenner advanced. A dark streak showed in the part in her hair and he had an idea that, stripped of makeup, she would never get past the preliminaries in a beauty contest. There was a permanent, ingrown look of boredom in her manner as she inspected him but that changed when she heard his name.

"Yes sir," she said, at once attentive. "Mr. Matlock's expecting you. You're to go right in, Mr. Fenner. The door at the end of the hall." At the same time she picked up the telephone, dialed twice and said, "Mr. Fenner is here."

The door that Fenner opened gave on a small anteroom with two desks, one on each side of the doorway beyond. A full-figured blonde with false eyelashes looked up from one, her smile quick and automatic. Tight-end Freddie sat at the other and now he stood up and preceded Fenner to the closed door. Knocking once, he opened it and said, "Fenner. Do you want me to stay?"

By then Fenner was past him and Matlock pursed his lips a moment, considering his caller with his small hooded eyes.

"You carrying, Fenner?" he asked finally.

"Nope."

"Wait outside, Fred. I'll buzz if I want you."

The office, while not especially large, was an improvement over the waiting room. Here everything looked genuine—the oversized divan and three matching chairs in dark-green leather, the walnut desk. There were two television sets, one portable and the other with a twenty-five-inch screen. There was also an all-band radio on one windowsill, three telephones, and a base with glass buttons, one of which showed a white light.

Maurie Matlock looked right at home in his high-back executive chair. With his nicely tailored, pin-stripe, dark-gray suit complete with vest, the white shirt and dark-blue tie; the French cuffs with the heavy gold links, the jowly but healthy-looking face, he could have been type-cast as a prosperous and successful businessman of fifty, which in a sense he was. When he was ready he pointed his cigar at a chair across from the desk, his little eyes hard and unfriendly as Fenner took it.

"So you had to get cute with me?"

"Cute?" Fenner said indifferently. "How?"

"With that envelope. We shake down your apartment and rip open your office file. I warned you this morning and you had it all the time."

"Wrong."

"What do you mean, wrong?" Matlock sat up. "You don't have it?"

"I told you."

"Then what the hell're you wasting my time for? You said—"

"I said I wanted to talk about it."

"So talk."

"I will. But first there's something else. A couple of murders. That's the only reason I'm in this. So let's talk about motive, okay? And those markers you've been holding on Bruce Townsend. That's the reason Ludlow came up with that hot stock, isn't it? You worked out a three-way deal—you and the New York boys and Townsend—right? Hot stock, worth maybe ten or twelve percent of market value if they find a sucker willing to buy. Against fifty or sixty percent of value for cold clean stock. Say two hundred grand. Half for New York, which nets them twenty-five percent; a hundred for you in exchange for your markers. Townsend makes the switch and he's off the hook once and for all."

The reaction to this surprised Fenner. Matlock's laugh was a humorless bark. He pointed the cigar and said, "It's a neat theory. It should have worked. Only right now Townsend's got those markers, all of them."

It was Fenner's turn to register surprise. He gave Matlock a quick bleak stare to be sure Matlock was not putting him on.

"Where'd he get them?"

"He isn't saying. My guess is he took them after he put two slugs in Les Ludlow's head."

"He didn't take the envelope."

"How do you know?"

"Because someone else did. Ludlow's girlfriend. But let's stick to the markers. How do you know Townsend has them?"

"I checked over a list he made of each and every marker I originally held before I made a deal."

"Deal?" Fenner's surprise was still mounting. "With him?"

"With that broad he left his wife for. The Latimer woman. And she's some tough chippie. She made a luncheon date with me this noon. At Locke Ober's, maybe afraid I might get rough. You want to know the terms?"

Fenner understood he was going to be told anyway so he sat and waited until Matlock was ready.

"I told her the fact that Townsend had swiped those markers didn't mean I couldn't lean on him hard. She admitted it—he must have told her the whole goddamned story—but she said if he was threatened she'd go to the law with the markers as evidence. With them the D.A. might get an indictment or two. Even if he didn't it would get around and raise a stink and that kind of publicity we don't need these days."

"She must have offered something."

"She did. She had it all figured out. . . . Funny," he said, digressing. "That Super Bowl bet was a one-time thing with me. I'd been out of the books for years but that one looked too good to pass up."

He hesitated, as though he needed a moment to dwell upon the happy result of his wager. "It's already paid an easy fifty plus in vigorish that Townsend got up from time to time. Very nice. The markers still out said he owed forty-six more plus the original thirty."

He leaned back, no longer watching Fenner. "So here's what she comes up with. Townsend writes off the fifty plus; that's gone. For the seventy-six he still owes—the bet plus vig—he'll give me a note for the original thirty on my promise to forget the forty-six and lay off."

To substantiate the statement he opened the center drawer and waved a piece of white paper at Fenner.

"With Townsend holding the markers I figured I'd better grab it. Strictly legit," he added. "For value received. Eighteen months at eight percent. With his signature, and the bank knowing it'll be paid when the old man goes, we can discount it just like any other business note. Which we will." He shrugged. "Of course we could still hassle him a bit, but we'll see." He returned the note to the drawer and leaned elbows on the desk. "So let's talk about that envelope. You've got to have an angle. Let's hear it."

Fenner looked the room over, his grin tight and humorless like his gaze. "You got a bathroom here?" When Matlock pointed to a closed door Fenner said, "You wanted to know if my office was bugged this morning. I'm taking no chances with you. So let's adjourn to the john, okay? It's big enough for two, isn't it?"

Matlock squinted at Fenner as if he were a block away. When he saw Fenner was serious he grunted and pushed his chair back, his expression one of open contempt.

Once the door of the bathroom closed an overhead ventilating fan started. This, Fenner knew, would make any microphone useless. When Matlock had lowered himself onto the turned-down toilet seat, Fenner pushed the shower curtain aside and perched on the edge of the tub.

"The New York crowd sent up the wrong man," he said, coming directly to the point. "Maybe it was Ludlow's fault, maybe not, but he blew it. It happened in your territory so that's not going to improve your relationship with New York. You've made your deal on the markers. The only thing the New York people can salvage now is the stock certificates they sent up here. They know they can't win them all but if they get that envelope back they haven't actually lost anything and they can start over."

Matlock nodded thoughtfully. "You figure pretty good, Fenner. What's your proposition?"

"I told you I never had that envelope, never saw a single certificate. I don't know exactly where it is now but it's still in town even though Ludlow's girlfriend has gone. It might take Freddie five minutes to locate it and bring it back."

"What do you get out of it, a cut?"

"No cut. What I want from you is a promise to forget all about Ludlow's girlfriend—and pass the word to your New York pals—and to stay away from me. I don't want to see any of your goons following me around or getting in my way."

Matlock thought it over. Fenner could almost see his mind work because Matlock understood that kind of a proposition. The gambler's eyes had taken on a half-open sleepy look and when he spoke there was somehow a soft sound of menace in his words.

"We could do it another way, Fenner. *You can be made to get that envelope.* Word got around you were kind of a hardnosed cop and I understand you know how to handle yourself. But I've got troops. You could get picked up some dark night; we might even make you tell us all about that envelope. So I'm wondering why I should make any deal."

"Because there's another way."

"Which is?"

"I've done a bit of insurance work," said Fenner, and this was the truth. What followed was not. "And I've been putting out feelers. Ten percent is the usual payment for recovery of stolen goods. The local law, and maybe the Feds, frown on the practice but it happens. So I figure I can get forty thousand for that envelope and no questions asked.

"So think about it, Maurie," he said. "If I go to the insurance people you're going to have to do one hell of a lot of explaining to your New York friends. They're going to be out four hundred large ones in stock and I don't think they're going to like it much. Or you either. The deal blew up. Maybe because of Ludlow, maybe not. And don't forget the foul-up happened in your territory. You had to be some sort of a middleman. Meanwhile I'll have forty grand to spread.

"The way I heard it you're a pretty successful businessman these days," he added. "Have been for several years; no problems with the law except some trouble with the I.R.S. You haven't even been booked in how long? Fifteen years?"

Matlock allowed himself a grin of agreement. "About that."

"Legitimate. No rough stuff lately, is the way I get it. Big in suburban condominiums. Or fronting for an outfit that is. A construction company that puts in contract bids that get accepted. But you've got associates here and there and I guess you could try to put me away if it was important enough. But is it?

"Because I've got a lot of friends too, Maurie. Not like yours but they get around just the same. And if you put out the word on me it will get back to me within hours and a guy has to protect himself. So what I'll have to do is spread the forty—if I go the insurance way—three or maybe four ways. For that kind of money I think I just might be able to get two or three of the best hit men in the East up here in no time at all. Pros who don't give a damn who they blast. I'll have all I'll need to take you out because I know where to find you and you can't hide and still stay in business."

It was a lot of talk for Fenner and he wasn't sure how much of it he meant. But then no one had ever put a contract out on him so he couldn't be sure. Also he had learned how to sound convincing, and poker-playing friends had difficulty knowing just when he was bluffing. Now he could see the change in the broad jowly face. The wide bald expanse was shiny with perspiration; so were the cheeks. The little eyes seemed busy with thought and no longer were there any signs of menace or contempt in his expression.

Fenner pressed him in the same direct, even tones. "You

thinking, Maurie? You going to make up your mind or do we close up shop now?"

"I've already made it up. Like you say, legit is better at my age. No heat, no trouble. So let's forget all about insurance companies, okay? . . . But you know something, Fenner? I heard you were a pretty straight-up operator. Friends on the cops and at headquarters and like that. If I take your offer, and I'm going to, you'll be compounding a felony, won't you?"

It was a problem Fenner had been weighing in his mind all during the slow, traffic-impeded ride. Never had he been in a situation remotely similar to this one. What he proposed bothered him greatly but his first obligation was to his client and he rationalized his decision as best he could.

"Morally you're right, Maurie. Legally I doubt it. If you never have a stolen object you can't be accused of receiving stolen goods. Once that envelope is in my hands I have no choice. I have to turn it in. And whose fault was it anyway? A broker sending out a messenger with three million in stock certificates like they were trading stamps."

He carried the thought a step further in his mind. The theft or recovery of stock he had never had or even seen was in reality none of his business. He had not earned the right to it. It had been a gift from a pretty young woman who happened to trust him and had no further use for it. And he had long ago learned that when things were none of his business it was best to keep as far away from such things as possible. What he said was:

"I want to nail whoever killed your man Ludlow and my friend Lipscomb, the stamp dealer. I don't want anything to get in the way until I do. I don't want any part of hot stock; I don't want any part of you and your boys. So this time I'm bending a little. Call it expediency, unless you've got a better word."

Matlock stood up and pulled down his vest. "Suppose that envelope isn't where you think it is?"

"Then we won't have a deal, will we?"

Matlock took a small breath, bunched his lips. "Okay, you've got my word." He offered his hand and Fenner took it, not happy about what he was doing but liking the alternative less. "So where do I send Freddie, and what does he have to do?"

Fenner took the key from his hip pocket and put it in Matlock's palm. "South Station. I think main concourse. Maybe you should send someone with Freddie," he added dryly. "Maybe you should go yourself."

He opened the bathroom door, started across the office, then stopped. He moved back toward Matlock, who had been following him, until their faces were about a foot apart.

"Just remember, Maurie," he said quietly. "I'm passing up forty thousand to stay out of trouble and keep things cool for me and that girl. If one of your boys—"

Matlock cut him off. "Forget it, Fenner. With me a deal's a deal." He gave a short bark which Fenner assumed was a laugh. "If anybody even bumps into you on the sidewalk just let me know"—he barked again—"and I'll have him taken care of."

19

THE GRAY MERCEDES 350 SL was no more than five minutes late when it angled slowly toward the curb in front of Laura Latimer's apartment. Jack Fenner, who had been leaning against a corner of the building, flipped away his cigarette, feeling the first drops of the predicted showers as he walked over to open the car door for the woman. She wore the same outfit he had seen in his office that morning and, ignoring his helping hand, slid, slim legs first, out of the small car. She straightened beside him and they stood mute and immobile in the scattered raindrops while Townsend pulled ahead to back into a parking space.

From the corner of his eye Fenner noted the tight red mouth, the fixed, straight-ahead, unblinking look in the dark eyes. Townsend's handsome features had the same strained, distant expression and he offered no greeting as he moved ahead to unlock the street door.

The silence continued until to Fenner it became a game with three players, the first one to speak being the loser— through the inner door and lobby, up the elevator; another door to be unlocked, a procession now, Fenner bringing up the rear like a well-trained dog at heel. The room needing some light, Townsend moved first to flip an electric switch and then click on a floor lamp near the divan.

By then the charade seemed silly but Fenner, the unwanted guest, felt he should play the game. When the woman disappeared into the inner hall as she had the night before, apparently heading for the bedroom, he made for the divan and plumped down in one corner. Trying to appear nonchalant and unperturbed, he waited for some gambit. This was the big man's prerogative and had to come eventually. He watched Townsend head for the kitchen and he was still sitting there when the man came back with a tray. Because good manners were part of Townsend's heritage even in difficult situations, there were three drinks, whisky-on-the-rocks by the look of them. Townsend took one for himself and sat down. When he indicated the tray, Fenner accepted the invitation and broke the silence.

"Thanks," he said, and reached for a glass.

Townsend nodded but kept his gaze averted until Laura returned. Again she had let down and combed her black hair, but now she wore a long quilted blue robe with pockets. She picked up the remaining drink and sat at the opposite end of the divan. She took a sip and then, holding her glass in both hands, gave Fenner a cold contemptuous stare and said:

"Well, Mr. Fenner, are you ready to tell us why we're here? Bruce said you sounded a bit threatening over the telephone."

"Threatening?" Fenner tipped one hand. "Maybe. What I had in mind was to tell you both what I found out the past twenty-four hours. I thought you might want to hear it before I go to the police."

"Well I think that's real considerate of you," she said with heavy sarcasm. "Wouldn't you say so, Bruce?"

This time Townsend looked right at Fenner. "All right, Jack. Let's get on with it. Just what do you want with us?"

Fenner took a swallow of Scotch and nodded absently as he groped for the proper opening. "I had a caller last night. The young woman who accompanied Leslie Ludlow up from New York."

He went on to explain why she had come and her hope to get half of the five thousand Ludlow was to be paid for completing the transaction.

"She waited outside my office in the car Saturday morning until she got worried about Ludlow. When she finally went upstairs she found him dead. She's not sure exactly why she emptied his pockets but she did; she also found the envelope full of stock certificates under Ludlow's raincoat."

He hesitated, watching Townsend and trying to read his mind. So far there had been no noticeable facial reaction, so he said:

"Now let's not kid about that stock business, Bruce. I've just had a talk with Maurie Matlock so I'm not guessing. It goes like this. A sort of three-way deal. Hot stock from an earlier New York theft of three million plus. To be exchanged by you for legitimate matching certificates from your vault. For the switch, you were to get your markers back. This much I know so there's no point in denying it. What I don't understand is *why* you agreed to such a deal.

"I know all about the markers," he added. "How much you already paid in vigorish, how much you still owe. But you were good for it, or would be when your father died. My guess is that Matlock was willing to let the debt pile up. What changed his mind, and yours? The only answer I can think of is that some kind of pressure forced you into removing that stock from the company inventory. What kind of threat was it?"

Townsend had been staring into his glass. When he glanced up his face seemed slacker, the blue eyes miserable.

"About ten days ago two men picked me up outside the club. One was black. He was the one with the gun. I'd never seen either of them but the gun was real enough. They forced me into the car and made me lie down on the floor. One drove and the other held the gun on me. I think we went down somewhere in the Blue Hills area. When they stopped we were on a dirt road way out in nowhere. The black told me to get out and when I did I heard him cock the revolver.

"Jesus, Jack!" he said, a touch of remembered horror clouding the blue eyes. "That bastard really had me scared silly. I mean it. I could feel my knees trembling. I could hardly stand when one of them told me to walk. I took about three steps, too scared to talk, just wondering when the first bullet would hit me."

He took a breath and blew it out noisily. "Then they told me to stop. I turned and the black wasn't pointing the gun any more. They told me to get back in the car. They said this was just a trial run to show me how easy it could be done. Then they told me what they wanted.

"They said Matlock needed his money, that he was tired of waiting for my father to die. They told me what I was to do. They gave me a list of all the stock certificates stolen in New York and said I was to check our inventory and see which ones I could duplicate. They said I was to get in touch with Matlock when I had the information, that if I refused to make the switch the next ride would be the last one. They drove to town with me on the floor. They let me out at the end of the subway in Forest Hills."

"So you called Matlock when you'd checked the inventory and told him what certificates you could provide."

"I had to," Townsend said, his voice little more than a whisper. "What else could I do? Go to the police? How long could they give me protection? Those two gunmen scared hell out of me."

Fenner could believe what he had heard and understand the very real threat Townsend had to face. It could well have been a genuine and deadly warning. Too many bodies had been found over the past few years in city alleys, in trunks of cars or gutters to discount such a threat unless one was better equipped to cope with it than an innocent like Bruce Townsend.

"Then it was you who picked my office for the meet," he said. "Why? You knew I'd be out of town but what's the rest of it?"

"I was afraid to meet Ludlow at any place he picked. I kept thinking he might get something on tape that he or someone else could blackmail me with later on. It was all right with

him. I told him I didn't have a key to your place but he said
that would be no problem, that he'd be there and waiting for
me when I came at ten-thirty."

"Did you go there with murder on your mind?"

"Would he tell you if he did?" It was Laura again but
neither man looked at her.

"With the firm's stock," Fenner pressed, "but with no
intention of swapping? Watching for a chance to shoot from
behind and get your markers? Ludlow must have carried them
as part of the deal."

For long seconds Townsend simply stared, mouth agape and
the color fading from his tanned face. He seemed temporarily
tongue-tied and spoke with difficulty.

"No, damn you!"

"You went to my building Saturday morning. The girl in the
first-floor travel agency can testify to that much."

"Who else says so?" Laura Latimer's dark gaze had a
malevolent quality and her voice was arrogant.

Fenner blinked, not quite understanding her attitude until
she continued in the same scathing tones.

"I can say Bruce had breakfast right here with me at
nine-fifteen Saturday morning. You want a menu—melon,
poached eggs on toast, coffee. He never left the apartment
until noon."

Townsend shook his head, defeat in every line of his body.
"No, Laura. You stay out of this. I don't want you perjuring
yourself. . . . Yes," he said to Fenner, "I was there. Ludlow
was on the floor. I could see the blood on the side of his face."

"Did she"—Fenner glanced at the woman—"know you
were going to meet Ludlow?"

"No."

"Or about the stock switch, or the markers?"

"Not until last night. She kept after me," he added, not
looking at her.

"You didn't take your markers from his body?"

"I didn't even touch Ludlow. I can't even remember how I

felt. Shocked and sick and sort of paralyzed, I guess. If I thought at all it was about the stock I'd brought, and how I had to get it back in the vault Monday morning before anyone discovered it was missing. I don't even remember getting out of there."

He hesitated, a look of awe and distance in his eyes, as though he could see once more the scene he was describing.

"I don't think my brain began to function until I was back in my car. I had to sit there a while because I was too shaky to drive. The only thing I could think of, the only explanation I could accept, was that some mob guy must have killed him, that maybe Ludlow had been working some double-cross. I didn't bother to ask myself why."

"But you wound up with those markers." Fenner took his time, facing the woman now, his green eyes steady under her icy glare. "Matlock told me about your lunch date today. He even showed me a legitimate and genuine note for the original thirty thousand. He told me about how much Bruce still owed in interest and how much he had already paid. He told me why he decided to settle. . . . You signed it?" he said to Townsend.

"It was Laura's idea. I didn't think Matlock would go for it but he did. She said it was worth a try and I was too fouled up mentally to argue. But I didn't take those markers from Ludlow."

"I believe you," Fenner said, recalling the first sentence in Hildy Dryden's hand-delivered letter. When he saw the look of disbelief in Townsend's eyes he went on to give a summary of his talk with Hildy the previous night.

"She admitted she took the envelope with the hot stock Ludlow brought from New York. She found it under his raincoat on my settee. She still had it. She only lied to me once. When I asked if she had taken your markers she said, 'What markers?' all open-eyed innocence. I didn't press.

"She sent me a note before she left town," he continued. "She said she had what she came for—twenty-five hundred bucks. There aren't too many Townsends in the phone book;

your name was on those markers. She got to you and made her proposition, right? Nearly eighty grand in markers for twenty-five hundred . . . If it comes to it the D.A. can get a court order to check your bank account; if you paid it will show up."

Townsend took another large breath and let it out slowly before he spoke, head hung, his voice a whisper of shame. "You're right, Jack," he said. "That's exactly what happened."

Fenner leaned back on the divan, his drink untouched. "So what have we got?" The question was rhetorical. "I told you the other day I had but one interest—to help find out who killed Fred Lipscomb, the stamp dealer. And not counting a possible mob job I had three possibilities. First, Ludlow's girlfriend. But once I'd talked to her I couldn't tag her with a believable motive. She came to town for one reason only: to get half of the five thousand Ludlow was to receive for completing the transaction, even if she had to drug him and steal it.

"You were next, Bruce, and when I began to find out things you had to be the most likely prospect. The markers, plus the thought that once you had them you wouldn't have to make any stock switch. But the more I learned the less I liked the motive. Because there was one more person unaccounted for seen entering my office building that morning," he said, and went on to tell about Saul Klinger and his seat in the window of the delicatessen.

"He couldn't tell if this person was a man or woman," he said. "A hippie type, is what he said. Long black hair and pants. Well, he could not have mixed up Ludlow's lady friend with this person because I watched her pack at the Starlight Motel Monday morning. She didn't even bring a pair of slacks.

"But you have slacks," he said, turning to Laura. "You wore them last night. When you comb out your black hair it's shoulder length. You say you knew nothing about the stock switch. I believe you. I don't think you even knew that Bruce was coming to my office—"

He never got a chance to finish. Bruce was on his feet,

sudden anger tightening his mouth and giving a threatening thrust to his jaw even as his fists clenched.

"Now just a goddamned minute, Fenner! If you're inferring that Laura had anything to do with this I'm going to throw you out of here on your ass, and don't think I can't."

Because he had half expected some such reaction Fenner sat right where he was and watched the woman. Nothing seemed to have changed in the smooth olive face but when she spoke she addressed Townsend, her voice curt and commanding.

"Sit down, Bruce! Go on now," she added when Townsend hesitated. "Let's hear what the man has to say. If I killed somebody shouldn't you know about it?" Then, ready for Fenner as Townsend resumed his seat, she said, "Tell us about it, Mr. Fenner. Why would I want to kill this man Ludlow when I didn't even know him?"

"Oh, I think you knew him all right, Miss Latimer," Fenner said. "I also think he was killed for personal reasons that had nothing to do with markers or hot or cold stock."

A small humorous smile was working at the corners of her mouth now but her self-control was remarkable. Only her voice was coolly contemptuous as she said:

"You must have something more than a wild guess; that's what it is, isn't it?"

"It is a guess," Fenner said. "But there's more."

"Like what?"

"I got some identification on Ludlow from the motel manager Monday morning. The police had already learned the same thing from fingerprints. The checking they did then was routine. Back to Cincinnati where he came from. How he worked as an investigator for a credit bureau, and married a woman from the same company, and how he got shot one evening by that woman, who was then Mrs. Leslie Ludlow.

"But Ludlow had a lot going for him that night," he added in the same even voice. "The small-caliber slug went right through him below the shoulder. When the doctors learned the wound was not serious, the judge reduced the charge for

Mrs. Ludlow and she was released on two thousand dollars' bail. By the time Ludlow was out of the hospital a week or so later Mrs. Ludlow had emptied their apartment and taken off."

Again Townsend started to protest but she cut him off in the middle of a word in that same crisp, insolent way.

"Well, that gives us a pretty good picture of Mr. Ludlow and his background," she said, the humorless smile fixed tightly on her mouth. "But how does it concern me?"

Fenner glanced at Townsend, who sat like a statue, his expression puzzled and uncomprehending. When Fenner saw he would have no further trouble from that direction he continued to the woman.

"Sometimes in my business a guy will get a brainstorm. That's what happened to me this morning. So I got in touch with an outfit in Cincinnati in my line of work. I talked to a man named Wilson and told him what I wanted. It was a simple job. He called me back before I saw Matlock and I made some notes."

He took a slip of paper from his pocket. "Ludlow's police record checked out just like Lieutenant Bacon had it. But cities and counties all over the country have departments of vital statistics—births, deaths, marriages. Say a woman needs a marriage certificate to prove something but she's lost or misplaced hers. She can write to the proper department and get a photocopy of the original. A license like that lists a lot of information—husband's name, age, place of birth, father and mother's names. Same for the prospective wife, plus her maiden name.

"Now I knew you were from Kentucky, Miss Latimer," he said, very formal now. "But to me Kentucky meant Churchill Downs, Louisville, Lexington; maybe because I've never been in the state. After I'd heard from Wilson I thought of something else and got out an atlas."

He chuckled abruptly, a dry deprecating sound. "You see, I remembered just enough of my high school geography to recall that the Ohio River makes a boundary for part of its length between Ohio and Kentucky, and Cincinnati is on the Ohio. You want to guess what I discovered?"

Again he hesitated. The woman's fixed smile remained little more than a grimace, but he could see new glints in the eyes, black now under the lashes, and what he saw was not pleasant to contemplate.

"You're going to tell us anyway," she said. "Get on with it."

Again he looked at Townsend. He was deliberately drawing out his explanation, careful not to hurry or accent his words, or make a direct accusation.

"Did Laura ever tell you where she came from in Kentucky?"

Townsend swallowed, a very confused man as his glance flicked to the woman and he pulled it back.

"She may have."

"Ever hear of a city called Covington? About sixty thousand. A good-sized percentage of the inhabitants work in Cincinnati. It's like a suburb. All you have to do is drive across one of the bridges. I understand that at certain hours of the morning and late afternoon traffic is bumper to bumper.

"Well, Mrs. Leslie Ludlow," he said, "was born in Covington as Laura Latimer. As his final inquiry Sam Wilson discovered that she worked for the same credit outfit as Ludlow. So I say Laura not only knew Ludlow but married him—and shot him before she took off, apparently for New York."

Townsend put it together then. He looked at the woman with awed, incredulous eyes for a long moment. But there was a commendable streak of loyalty in him and this was someone who had so infatuated him with her charms and her scheming that he had deliberately left a wife who loved him.

"That doesn't prove a goddamned thing," he said finally but without total conviction. "Suppose everything you told us is true—"

"It is true."

"—suppose she was Ludlow's wife, suppose she shot him a long time ago. All right. She knew him and she lied about it. If you've got one shred of hard evidence that says she shot him in your office let's hear it."

"I don't have to prove anything, Bruce. That's not my job. I haven't any what you call hard evidence. But since I have to guess a little, I'd say he ran into her sometime earlier when he was in town. He found out she had set things up for a pleasant future with you and, being the kind of a guy he was, saw a way to collect, perhaps indefinitely if he wasn't too greedy."

He sighed and stood up. "With what I can give the police, what I have to give them—the only reason I came here was to let you know what was coming—they are going to concentrate. You've heard how much I've been able to come up with in the last couple days. What the law enforcement agencies in New York and Cincinnati can uncover with their resources when they really start digging ought to be enough so the D.A. can get an indictment on one charge or another. All I do now is dump what I have in Lieutenant Bacon's lap."

He glanced around and located the telephone. "Okay to use the phone? Bacon ought still to be in his office."

He had the handset off its cradle, but before he could begin to dial, Laura Latimer stopped him, her voice high-pitched and deadly.

"Put that down!"

Fenner stiffened into momentary immobility, not a muscle moving but his brain working furiously. For he had a very good idea of what he would face when he turned. His sixth sense, developed as a police officer and investigator, had, with the evidence he had received that afternoon, convinced him that his hunch was right.

The things he had said during the past half-hour, his exposition and his information, had been the truth. He also knew, and Townsend's challenge pointed up that fact, that he had no conclusive proof to support his contention. What he had hoped to do was force the issue, to make the woman take the final step that would reveal her true character—and her guilt. It was, he knew, a gamble, a risk he had to take if he was to accomplish his task. For he thought he understood now why she had changed to a dressing gown with pockets.

His phone call to Townsend demanding this confrontation, his hint of some police action, had surely been passed along to Laura. And given her history and background, added to his own assessment of her character, he was further convinced that she would never surrender voluntarily while there was still a chance, however improbable, for freedom. If true, there was only one method open to her.

He knew as though he had already seen it that when he turned there would be a gun in her hand. Her shrill command, its frightened urgency, seemed to promise that much; all he could hope for was that it would be the little .25-caliber murder weapon. So far he had guessed right. To create a reaction she could believe, he concentrated on appearing not only shocked and surprised but fearful. This last, he decided as he replaced the handset, would not be all that difficult. With a woman like Laura holding a gun he could get hurt, perhaps fatally.

But it was Townsend who spoke first, gaining some respite for Fenner. He had come out of his chair, and as Fenner eyed the little automatic Townsend said:

"Good Christ, Laura! Where'd you get that?" He sucked air and his voice was ragged. "What do you think you're doing?"

"Shut up, Bruce!"

The fierce compulsion in the cadence of her voice stopped him. He seemed to recoil like a child unjustly slapped in the face.

"I need a drink," she said. "You'd better get one for yourself while you're at it. You're going to help me and you're going to need it. . . . You," she said, tipping the muzzle at Fenner, "go back and sit down right where you were."

20

THE ROOM SEEMED unnaturally quiet as Jack Fenner very carefully came back to his corner on the divan. Not until he had leaned forward to lift his glass from the coffee table and take another small sip did Bruce Townsend pick up the other two glasses from the drink tray and turn slowly toward the kitchen, his expression stunned and uncomprehending, his movements those of a well-programmed automaton.

It was Fenner's move and he knew it. What he had to do was talk, not only to gain time until he could figure out the odds, but to make her respond and reveal to Bruce Townsend the real character of the woman who had kept him infatuated over the past several months. He watched the man return and carry his drink back to his chair. When Laura picked up her own glass with her left hand and perched on the far arm of the divan Fenner said:

"You've got the edge, Laura. So let's lay the rest of it out in the open. You say you didn't know about the stock switch, or that Bruce was going to meet Ludlow in my office Saturday morning. I believe you. Which has to mean that Ludlow made a date with you, figuring to have your little chat before Bruce showed up. Am I right so far?"

There was no answer to this. She seemed now to have

forgotten Townsend. She sipped her drink daintily but the eyes that stared back at Fenner were like black quartz, bright, cold, and inhuman.

"So Ludlow must already have known something about you before this trip. He must have been in town earlier, spotted you somehow and checked you out; found out how it was with you and Bruce and what kind of a future you'd have when his wife gave up and got the divorce. Ludlow told you he had never divorced you, that the charge of felonious assault—or whatever they called that shooting in Cincinnati—was still on the books, that the bail bondsman was still looking for you, that once Ludlow gave the word you had no future. So what did he want? Blackmail of some sort but not just some monthly payment because you didn't have that kind of money. How was he going to collect?"

The monologue, a combination of fact and fiction, finally produced the desired results. He got a response.

"You guess good, Fenner," she said. "Is there more?"

"Just a little background to set the record straight. Your marriage to Ludlow way-back-when was a flop. You tried to kill him and missed."

"He had it coming, the sonofabitch!" she said, her actress's accent forgotten. "I knew a month after we were married he was cheating. He was spending money on his harem while I kept working to pay the rent and buy the groceries. So this one night I walk in on him; he even had the bitch in my own bed. I might never have remembered the gun if he'd tried to apologize. But, oh no! Not Leslie. While the bitch was getting dressed he laughed about it and I started screaming at him and then I remembered the gun and I used it. If I'd been a better shot I'd have killed him and her too and pleaded diminished capacity or something."

"So you got lucky and took a reduced charge and low bail," Fenner said. "You went to New York and clawed your way up. A waitress first, right? A garment model who entertained important out-of-town customers for a fee so you could study acting. Bit parts in off-Broadway productions until you got a small chance in a major production. A week's tryout here in town, an introduction to Bruce."

He took a breath, still holding that bright steady gaze. "And here finally was what you wanted. A handsome, well-educated, society-type guy ripe for a woman like you who knew how to excite him. Good family, a trust fund in a couple of years—you couldn't know about the Matlock business—an interest in a well-established brokerage business."

He paused again, spacing his words. "Then Ludlow shows and demands a cut in the action. What the hell did he expect? Was he going to wait until you finally got Bruce away from his wife for good? I doubt it, Laura. I doubt it very much."

For the first time there was a break in her bright cold stare. Her eyes flicked to Townsend, who sat unmoving in his chair, a man still in shock; then down at the diamond solitaire.

"This," she said, and turned her hand so Fenner could see the stone. "He came to town two weeks earlier so someone could point out Bruce to him, so he would recognize him this trip. And we were having dinner and Leslie saw me. A couple of days later he was waiting for me when I came out of our office building. We went to a bar and he told me how it was. . . . You want the details?"

"Just the punch line."

"When he found I couldn't pay in cash he said the ring would do. I could think it over. I could give it to him when he came back. Over the weekend he could have a paste made that Bruce would never suspect. If Bruce noticed I wasn't wearing the ring I could say the stone had come loose and I was having it fixed. Then he phoned Friday afternoon. He didn't tell me why he was in town. Just where and when to meet him."

"You didn't know Bruce would be meeting him later?"

"How could I? Would I have gone there if I'd known Bruce might walk in on me? I thought Leslie wanted the diamond, period. And that would be just the beginning."

"But you knew what you were going to do."

"What choice did he leave me? He was on that settee in your office when I walked in and he had that same sneering grin I hated so much; like that last night in our bedroom. I got behind him. I didn't know what his job was but I knew he worked for some New York mob. I wanted to make it look like just another mob killing. I didn't see any envelope. I didn't know about the markers."

"And when you stepped back into the hall there was Mr. Lipscomb. Where was he?"

"In the doorway across the hall. I got out so fast I was still putting the gun in my bag." She shrugged off the thought, no pity or remorse showing since to her it had been a simple, cold-blooded job that had to be done.

"And that's the gun." It was not a question.

"And you want to know something funny? Leslie gave it to me right after we were married. I sometimes had to work evenings and there were a lot of local muggings."

Fenner wondered if she realized that the little gun was the conclusive proof the district attorney needed. As he considered his next step, Townsend came to life. Putting his glass aside, he stood up and faced the woman, his blue eyes sick and discouraged but a grim purposeful set to his jaw as he addressed her.

"What in God's name do you expect to do with that?" he demanded with mounting consternation.

"What do you think, you idiot?" she said, as though the answer was too obvious for debate. "What choice have I got? What choice did I have once Leslie showed up? He would never have let go and I fought too goddamned hard to get where I am to have him ruin it all. That little man across the hall? It was just his bad luck. Do you think I'm going to spend the rest of my life behind bars? . . . You don't have to do a thing but help carry him out when it gets dark," she added on a note of rising desperation. "You're big and husky enough for that, aren't you?"

She watched Townsend shake his head wearily and tried again, pleading a little now, the voice less strident.

"Or we can wait until dark and take him out and go for a ride. All you have to do is help me get him downstairs and into the car. You don't have to go. I'll make him drive."

"No, Laura. That's not the way. Give me the gun and I'll hold Jack. Maybe I owe you that much. If I get charged with being an accessory of some kind I can stand it. Take what cash you have here and what I have on me and run for it."

"No! How far would I get?"

Fenner cleared his throat to get some attention. "Better listen, Laura. A top attorney might do some plea bargaining; you might be out in six or eight years."

He might have said more but just then Townsend took a slow forward step and for the first time Fenner felt real fear, the sudden vacuum in his gut, the prickly scalp, the cold sweat starting. Because he realized now, beyond any doubt, that if Townsend crowded her she would fire.

It was not just instinct or intuition that convinced him; it was the blank, half-mad look in her eyes. And he had learned long ago that many women, once motivated and determined to kill, were more vicious, pitiless, and compassionless than men. To try reasoning with Laura in such a state would be futile. For she was now a cornered animal, her mind warped by fear, the need for survival bordering on hysteria.

When Townsend took another slow step he extended a hand, a father asking a simple favor from a backward child. With this the woman stood up. When she put down her drink Fenner knew he had to act. He had always expected to make some attempt to neutralize that little gun, but he had been working toward more favorable circumstances, a time of his choosing.

Now his position was an awkward one. He was still on the divan, the glass in his hand, the narrow wood coffee table diagonally in front of him.

Townsend was to his left and perhaps ten feet from Laura as

she stepped around the end of the coffee table to face him. That put the coffee table between her and Fenner and while he was trying to plan the proper move Townsend took still another step.

"Stay there, goddamn you!" This time the voice had a ring of utter panic. "I'll shoot! I will! If you take one more step."

Townsend seemed not to have heard. His handsome face was chalky, every muscle tense. But he still had the manner of a man in a trance who had become horrified by a situation beyond all comprehension.

Fenner could almost see him deciding on that next step. When he sensed some new tensing of Laura's finger on the trigger of that gun, the final preparation that came before squeezing off a shot, he made his move.

"*Laura!*"

The single word was so loud and unexpected, so sudden and imperious, that it distracted her for one all-important instant. In that watch-tick of time Fenner tossed his drink, not the glass, just the half-melted ice cubes, the whisky and water.

The mixture splashed directly over her face, bringing a momentary blindness. In almost the same continuous movement he flipped the wooden coffee table upward and over.

The gun went off just as the upset table hit her at the knee and before she could decide where to aim. As she staggered to regain some balance and blinked to clear wet eyes, Fenner hurdled the overturned table. The final shot exploded as he slapped hard at her wrist.

He saw the gun spin from her hand. Then he was close and she was shrieking incoherently and trying to claw at him and he grabbed a wrist and spun her violently toward the divan. He watched her body slam against the cushions and bounce back, her head snapping forward. He had a quick glimpse of the bewildered, wide-open eyes in the wet face. Then she slowly bent still more, spread fingers covering her face as her black hair fell forward, feet flat on the floor, her forearms resting on her thighs in a near-fetal position.

21

IT WAS ALL OVER as suddenly as it began. For what seemed like five minutes but in reality could not have been more than five seconds Fenner stood motionless, gaze fixed on the woman. The only sound in the room was the thudding of his heart and her harsh, tortured breathing.

She did not cry, or even sob, and those breathing sounds came more from frustration and defeat than from pain, a reaction to the madness that had consumed her. When he stooped to recover the gun he was aware of wet palms and the leaking of perspiration from armpits down his sides, a noticeable weakness at knees that felt none too steady. With a long and audible sigh of relief he turned to Townsend, who seemed not to be aware of what had happened but stared with dead eyes and without comprehension at the bent figure on the divan.

He did not even move when Fenner spoke to him, so Fenner took him by one arm, applied enough force to turn him, and led him back to his chair. When he pushed, Townsend sat down weakly and Fenner picked up the half-empty glass from the floor where the big man had put it.

As Townsend accepted it Fenner watched the color seep back into the cheeks and could see a growing sense of awareness. Fenner still didn't know, would never know, what made a man like Townsend tick or understand why he had not heeded the woman's warning. Was it courage? Some unshakable reckless confidence in himself? Simple stupidity? Or the absence of imagination of one unable to know the difference between a threat and stark reality.

"Drink up, Bruce," he said. "I'll fix another. For me too. I spilled mine."

Townsend nodded, the blue eyes focusing at last. He offered the glass. When Fenner returned with fresh drinks he bent over, hands on kneecaps and began to speak, a counselor trying to give new reassurance to a defeated friend.

"It's going to be a rough couple of hours, Bruce. I'll make some calls. We'll have to go down to headquarters and have it out with Lieutenant Bacon—he'll be here in a few minutes—and some assistant D.A. . . . Are you listening?"

When he saw Townsend nod he said, "I don't think this stock-switch business will have to come up. It had nothing to do with the murder. You put the firm's stock back. You're really not guilty of anything but bad judgment in falling for a woman like Laura."

Townsend did not question or resent the last statement. His mind on other things, he said, "The intent was there."

"If they jailed people for intent they couldn't build enough cells."

"I'll have to tell Alan and my father," Townsend said, unable to wipe out his feeling of guilt.

"Okay." Fenner gave Townsend's shoulder a squeeze as he straightened. "But not now. Not until you get your head together."

"She would have shot me." The words were hushed, incredulous. "If you hadn't—" He broke off, as though seeking some confirmation. "Wouldn't she?"

"Probably."

"I really thought she loved me," he said, a totally shaken man unable yet to acknowledge the truth.

"You're not the only one who has made the same mistake. You put yourself in a spot and lucked your way out of it so make the best of it. Your father will come around once he knows you're finished with Laura. And Caroline had the good sense to understand that even a simple-minded guy like you would eventually learn the score. I guess the most amazing thing is that she still loves you, but don't ask me why."

Having delivered his opinion and his gratuitous platitude, Fenner turned away to find that the woman on the divan had not moved; only her breathing had quieted. Aware that he would have no further trouble from that direction he stepped over to the telephone.

It took him a while to reach for it because he had a little head-straightening of his own to do. When he glanced at his watch and saw that it was only six o'clock he found it hard to realize that so much had happened in so short a time.

He knew what to expect from Bacon and the man from the district attorney's office; he had survived such sessions before. The problem bothering him now was what he was going to do *after* that session. It would be well past eight again before he would be free, again too late to make any kind of date. It occurred to him then that his love life, such as it was, was suffering. Here it was three solid days—and part of the night—on this one case. The weekend at Falmouth had started Friday. That meant he had neither seen nor phoned either of his two lady friends in a week.

For one crazy moment he found his imagination fantasizing. The subject of that aberration was Hildy Dryden. If only she were still in town an evening spent with her could, he felt sure, be a lot of fun even for a man fifteen years her senior. . . . So much for fantasy!

Well, there was still Kent Murdock. Maybe. He could try to locate him after he had called Bacon. He could promise a story and maybe a picture or two. If he also promised dinner, Murdock might stick around—unless of course *he* had a date. Later they could go to his or Murdock's place for some drinks and some music. Oldies with Art Tatum and Herman Chittison; with Bobby Hackett and Jack Teagarden. Maybe a couple of new ones with Ruby Braff and Hank Jones, or Dick Hyman. Maybe Yank Lawson's group or Count Basie on "Sweet Lorraine." . . .

With a muttered curse at such daydreaming, he dialed and requested an extension. He asked the detective that answered if Lieutenant Bacon was still around.

"He's got his hat and coat on," the man said. "I think he's on his way home."

"Well, grab him. Tell him it's Jack Fenner. Tell him I think it's important."

As the silence came and he waited for the lieutenant's voice he was glad he had already made that second drink. When he had time he'd call young Lipscomb and give him the word. It was always gratifying to be able to report good news to a client; to know you had done a proper job and really earned your fee.

A NOTE ABOUT THE AUTHOR

GEORGE HARMON COXE was born in Olean, New York, and
spent his youth there and in nearby Elmira. After a year at
Purdue and one at Cornell, he worked for five years with
newspapers in California, Florida, and New York, and did
advertising for a New England printer for five more. Since
that time he has devoted himself to writing—for two years
with Metro-Goldwyn-Mayer, then as a free-lance, selling
numerous short stories, novelettes, and serials to magazines
as well as to motion-picture, radio, and television producers.
He is a past president of the Mystery Writers of America,
and winner of its Grand Master Award in 1964.

A NOTE ON THE TYPE

THIS BOOK was set by computer in Laurel, a face based on Caledonia, a Linotype face designed by W. A. Dwiggins. It belongs to the family of printing types called "modern face" by printers—a term used to mark the change in style of type letters that occurred about 1800. Caledonia borders on the general design of Scotch Modern, but is more freely drawn than that letter.

THE BOOK was composed, printed and bound by The Colonial Press Inc., Clinton, Massachusetts.